Red

RBGW SERIES

Hands

ISIS MELANTHA

This book is dark romance and crime fiction, so I highly recommend it to enjoy the content like that only.

Editor 1: Halima T.

Editor 2: Ophelia (hor.crux3)

Coverdesign: Leona (design.the.pages)

Character & Couple Art: Taesha (digital_artist_taesha)

To those who have lost love for themselves gradually over time.

Always remember, love was expensive, you are priceless, and those who couldn't afford to give you were poor. It wasn't your fault.

TRIGGER WARNING

The contents of the book are dark and not for the audience, uncomfortable with triggering situations, such as graphic violence, arson, pyromania, self-harm, death, suicide, anxiety, murder, secret society, consensual-non-consensual, non-consensual, dubious consent, abduction/kidnapping, and explicit sexual situations, etc.

There are also descriptive mentions of kinks such as period sex, fire play, ice play, primal play, blood play, bondage, degradation, etc, but not limited to. I will highly advise you to consider your mental health before diving into this book.

PLAYLIST

Under the influence - Chris Brown
Agora Hills- Doja Cat
Pretty Girl- Maggie Lindemann
Beautiful Ghosts- Taylor Swift
Alone, Pt.II- Alan Walker, Ava Max
She- Selena Gomez
Sad Forever- Jada Facer
Angel Baby- Troye Sivan
Call It What You Want- Taylor Swift
Wonderland- Neoni
Beautiful- Michele Morrone
Die For You- The Weekend, Ariana Grande

PROLOGUE

Winters in London are beautiful but hard to breathe. The seeping cold shrivels my inside, and my brain chants one descriptive monologue about hot chocolate and its advantages. The sentiment will be common among sexy accents, if not the smell of the home we carry or the aroma of coffee, or the sophisticated tradition of tea and cookies. But today, it lingers peculiarities in my nose, and not enough to calm my stress that I could feel bubbling beneath my skin.

I was supposed to meet my father today. We had a date, and he promised to be there, at least until yesterday's dinner, when he beamed with happiness and his favourite wine in one hand. Guess what? He betrayed me for an official meeting with his office mates—in the end, having Mayor as a Dad acted against my ambition. He promised he'd take me to many of the musicals held in Royal Albert Hall because socialising in high society in elite venues comes as a perk of being in holding status.

Tonight is one of those days where I eagerly waited to be his priority, for him to fulfil his pending promises that top the mountain of many broken ones. He gracefully failed because his work occupied most of his time.

I ditched both his chauffeur and the tickets his secretary had left for me, and paid for everything out of my own pocket.

Bustling crowd. Flickering lights on streets and people gathered to have the most of it before the twentieth December arrives pricks at the memory of my mother who once made sure family dinners and quality outings were important. As Christmas and New Year get closer, from fifteen onwards, settles with a different colour of anxiety. The presence of two hands ticking and stealing something from me makes me vulnerable. It did then, too, when I was waiting for my mother outside the operation theatre where she died with my baby sister, who never got to see the light of the day.

I bite the corner of my lip, shaking the heaviness inside my chest, and swallow a bittersweet taste in my mouth. I am not a crybaby and never have been one. Supposedly, my mother said she had a hard time with me because I wouldn't act like other babies or even when I grew up a little, I still didn't act like other kids my age. It so happens that she never thought I'd be born with a gift at the stake of not leading a normal childhood.

Carving the frosty clouds of my breath, I hummed the moonlight sonata, the piano in my mind, and the keys magically against my fingers strummed as I played it through my imagination. I forgot I was walking when my fingers picked the rhythm of the keys in the air. The tune bounced against my fingers, and the cold breeze surrounding the night in the deadly silent winter echoed the voices of the music notes in my head.

Slowly, I detached my existence from the people passing by on the late December night and became one with the notes.

The voice in my head on the highest volume and the broken fairytale musical came into existence. A smile plastered on my face, and the thrill pounded inside my chest, replacing the feeling that moments before put me down in a not-so-great headspace. My entire body hummed with the notes. I was no longer an existence of my own. Everything of me became that of the music, whispering through my lips and flowing in my head. The melancholic charm with the strings of anticipation raised goosebumps on my skin.

The mesmerising heartbreak was about to strike me with the next note...

"ARHHHH!"

The flow shattered. Ripped from the roots of music, my notes fell blank in the steady air of the isolated street that I've hardly any knowledge of entering. Although, I know whom to blame for this mishap of trudging on the wrong street. None other than my noble self. Oh, now Dad will be royally pissed finding me not at home before dinner.

"ARGHHH..."

A scream. It was the same that broke my concentration. Another step and red hands grabbed my shoulders from behind. The realisation of the red being blood made my vocal cords act fast. I shouted, brushing off those hands in haste and running to where the road led me.

However, my attempt failed. The hand that held onto my shoulders now grabbed my leg, pulling me towards it.

I panicked. Every sensibility died in my vision. The push and pull, back and forth, levered a corrupted fear suffocating me. I tried kicking for the sake of my safety despite the futile efforts, and yet, tumbled, falling face-first into the thick layer of snow. My breath heavy, and my limbs ached. Fingers buried in the snow, I clawed on the ground and tried dragging myself against the pull.

"Help me." The voice of the person screamed.

"In the name of the god, the Mary, and holy spirits, fucking I need the help here the most!" I kicked at the hand holding me from the other foot.

"Help me." A feminine voice, I inferred, kept repeating the same thing.

In a state of panic, I felt weak. So weak that the sensation of hands holding my leg turning cold stood as an expensive act of a period murder movie.

Just to be able to see the possie of the woman and myself, I forced my head to the side and saw a man dragging the bleeding woman away from me. He held her by the hair, and when his eyes fell over me from his shoulder as he turned to take a glance at my helpless self, I paled.

The dead eyes, the features, and even if the resemblance of

physique doesn't stand the same, I know him. He died ten years ago. If not for his scanty clothing and skin nearly turning blue terrified me, the burn mark that stood out from his cause of death did. Half of his face was covered in them, brutally burned. I could see the rough healing and his teeth from the side.

I wanted to scream. I desperately wanted to call someone. All I could do was see a dead man dragging the woman in front of me and stabbing her multiple times until her blood turned the white snow red. It trickled. The warm liquid gushed thick in the freezing white. At that moment, even I knew she was no more.

When he was done with her, my death appeared closer than I anticipated. I expected him to kill me next, but it never happened. He dipped his hands in the dead lady's blood and walked to the wall of the store that was closed. He started vigorously writing something. Every time the blood dried off his hands, he'd return, dip his hands wet in blood again till covered red, and then go back and write on the wall.

I silently witnessed a dead man's action until I couldn't.

CHAPTER ONE

What is it that appeals to everyone about the new guy in town? The appeal doesn't grant me the enlightenment. Maybe everything has got to do with my good looks and unforgettable personality that's plenty hedonist, not to mention the fact that the captain of the football team of the college I entered into happens to be my best friend.

Rumours fly fast. In a college like this, where the halls are filled with old money and over-achievement, the city's new deputy commissioner of police's son joining in makes sense. It drags attention. Unwanted eyes that expect you to stand out and hawk every step taken. Things don't happen because they're bound to happen. It does because the initiator decides that silent breathing and common lives don't sit well with peace. Anarchy, that's the term. My personal favourite in the dictionary of pretty violent and strokes of black and red.

I had many things to look forward to with my parents moving to London. One of those said, my parents purposely moved with me to London from a town in Wales because it was time they returned to where their stems dug their roots.

My father moved there two decades before to support my maternal grandfather until he departed last year. For my Dad, a renowned officer, it only took a serial murderer put behind bars, and coming from the lineage of lawyers, officers, and any job that marked Spades as the legacy of law meant something.

Spade has a presence in high society. It mattered, carried a weight, and rested on our shoulders. My cousins wreaked havoc in courts daily as their habitual tea drinking. My uncles jacked politics in their nerves as narcotics, and my aunts were figures of people's great representations and voices in the media. If that wasn't enough, the remaining people in my family served as institutions of law and policymakers overseas. However, carrying the surname of Spade isn't often enough because family dinners turn into a competitive game where every member weighs their achievement as if it were a bank balance.

We make Spade the top of the game. We are from the bloodline that carries an ace of all aces. We must keep on working as we mean what being Spade is, are some of the words my grandfather, uncles, and father has relayed.

In a decent play of power and brain, the pros of Dad's Sherlock Holmes act, his application for transfer with a promotion on top happened faster than a rat up a drain pipe, and the cons, he denied me from moving out until I got settled in the new place, despite him already buying an apartment for me.

I quote his warning, "We know you little violence gone wrong. If you're left to your own devices, I'd have to visit my son in jail, and we wouldn't like the sound of a father arresting his son. Stay with us until you turn 21 and your probation period is over."

It's not solely his money, to begin with. Unlike my other family members, I have a mother who works as a branch director of Leon Mutual Funds and Investment company. She was the happiest with the shift and paid for the sum I couldn't come up with. This significantly accounts for the contribution done by me. I earned from tutoring brats of his colleagues and higher-ups for five continuous years, and while that shit could pay well if you know what you're doing, I had done some other petty work and some freelancing website designs to make up for the remaining sum since Dad made it clear, he'd pay only a quarter and the rest is for me to come up with.

He bought a nice apartment in Mayfair which is currently unreachable because my father dearest holds complete authority over my finances. Just a month more, and I'll be owning my assets. Not to forget, I am a trust fund baby.

"I thought you'd not come," Hunter spoke, sitting next to me in his college football team jersey and shorts on the bleachers where I waited for him, ignoring the female and male attention I was getting from the sidelines.

"Guess what... Your face does turn me on," I said with an unapologetic face, and his was an epic proportion of annoyed. He downright hated my remarks and said, I intentionally do that to annoy people. *He is right there.*

"Are you joining the basketball team? If so, I suggest you go to the court. They're having trials today for the captain and team for the new season." He suggested, picking up his duffle bag dropped by his leg.

"They'd take me in from the looks of my face alone; undervalued like yourself are the people who go for the trials." I grinned wide when Hunter fisted his hand, ready to beat me to a pulp akin to our younger days.

His mother and mine were friends until she married some rich guy from the wrong side of London and moved away. She did travel back for summer vacations and that's how we boys got together.

Initially, Dad hated his mother for choosing the wrong people, but when she and her husband died years back from now, a lot changed. It changed Hunter, their profound mix of dirty, arrogant, rational thinker and foul player. Of course, one of the most important facts of inherited sin is him being the child of the god.

He does prayer services sometimes in the local churches, and while for my parents and the world, what a prosperous existence he is, who have come to adore him, I know the real face of this anarchy that took birth. He is a beast, and anyone sane couldn't stand by his side; that's why my hedonistic soul loves his deviant one.

"Let's change the ratio of your features. Then you'd love to go for the trials, bastard." He growled, and I shot to my feet, ready to throw back some punches and get in the gear for the nightly fun our parents never knew. For them, we were boys who loved playing together in the mud, only if the mud in the fields wasn't caused because we burned houses or people.

The wrong kind of people, definitely. While Hunter could be set on the path to devour the right kind in unforeseeable circumstances, I have chained myself for a less devastating side and a more lawful one.

My father should never come to know his son is an arsonist.

In my defence, I couldn't help. I loved fucking with fire from a very young age, even before I met Hunter. Once, I burned my mother's dresses, and she thought it was done by some criminal on lose, and that hardly was proven. My father's job gave me relaxation in many ways he'd never know.

I thought with time, I'd relinquish my interest in the burning agony, but I never did. It grew. It went wild when I wished to chain it until my mother saw me trying to burn nearly anything that I could get my hands on and forced me behind the doors of a therapist. The result of various tests, I am a person compelled to set fires to satisfy psycho-sexual cravings that can be greater than other forms of criminal paraphilia. In simple terms, diagnosed with pyromania. Now, I roam with a lighter in my pocket to keep myself chained.

As if it could.

"Are you coming, or should I leave you here?" Hunter hollered.

Disappointed that he wouldn't fight, I whipped out my lighter, flipping the guard, as flames levelled high in the air and made me smile. I fucking love it.

"Isn't it pretty, fucker?" I grinned wide, closing the lock and keeping it back in my pants pocket.

"Your lighter's upgraded to a flame thrower, I see. How long does this one last?" He ruffled his walnut brown hair, an element that reminds me of his mother, who was a sweet church girl I heard from stories until she met his father. How she was still able to remain sweet in his world blows my mind.

"More than you could ever in bed." I clicked my tongue, trotting beside him.

He brought me to the basketball court inside one of the old buildings of St. Evelyn University. It stood here for generations with prestige for both its great architecture and the golden graduates it produced. At the very least, my mother told me I'd be studying with Hunter after my first year of college—right before she dropped the brochure and information in front of me.

She thinks with Hunter on my side, she could keep track of my vandalism, only if she could see what her saint Hunter does behind closed doors with the name of his god involved.

"Do you even last, or pussy knocks you in first breath?"

"Fear the god's wrath, motherfucker." He pushed past the open doors and brought me to the middle of the court, where the coach had the boys lined in a semi-circle, each answering their roll call.

"I fear that guy enough to use his name without putting a swear word just fine." Winking, I walked to the man in his mid-thirties, ignoring the piercing glare of Hunter's central blue-brown heterochromatic orbs. Unlike my stark whiskey ones, which appear mischievous, his stands on the more intimidating end of the spectrum.

"Owen, how come you're here?" The man looked behind me at my brawny whore.

"Brought my friend for the trials, Baldwin. He transferred here this semester." Hunter informed, and the man gave me a once-over before smirking. What the fuck was it for?

"The smirk doesn't suit you, but your name does, Baldwin." I grinned, and everyone started laughing. The guy was pissed.

"Don't make him mad, bastard!" Hunter warned from behind.

Rolling my eyes, I joined the semi-circle as the guy took my name down on the register in hand. He eyed me several times throughout the trial speech he did. I had a wild urge to burn him.

I restrained until out and away from the eyes of a witness.

Only fools believe violence makes them look cool, whereas, in reality, it doesn't. Violence done for fun only makes arseholes, but purpose, it drives the madness to a much darker corner which gives meaning to everything. A madness worthy of the craziest anarchy and feeds the rebellious souls.

I checked the arena, ignoring the arse-long speech. Nothing seemed wow to me, however, it is much bigger than the one I attended back in the college during my first year in Wales.

Drifting from the cheerleading squad who practised on the

far corner, their eyes completely drawn to their steps, some exceptions were staring in our direction, too, I zoomed my eyes on the gates that opened to what seemed like a supply room behind them.

It was hard to decipher much from the distance. By the open gates, there was a net with basketballs in it. Must be out for the trials that'd begin and end soon if this shining head ended early with his performance speech.

Something caught my eye, or specifically, a girl. She had her long hair in a ponytail, with high-waist jeans, vans, and a crop top filming her frame. A simple girl to look but her motives don't appear to be one.

She stepped closer to the net with balls and pulled something out from her back pocket. One ball after another, I watched as she used something to cover the balls before her eyes discreetly looked my way. I couldn't see her face or features yet evident as the day; her intentions meant ill. The moment she saw me staring at her, flinching, she pulled back and ran away.

I said nothing. I did nothing. I just saw her running away from the supply to the other door. Probably, the backdoor, and she disappeared.

Once the Bald-loser finished, he went to grab a ball from the same basket I saw the girl standing by.

"What the fuck?! Ruth!! Someone, help. Who the fuck did this?" Bald-loser started shouting in the back until I was forced to go along with the other boys to see what his shiny head burned with the sun's rays.

Nearly everyone gathered and watched his hand stuck to the basketball. I snickered, watching his attempt, lively ones, to free himself. Now I know what she applied on the balls. Fucking superglue.

"It won't come out, coach. We have to take you to the infirmary," said one of the guys before he started escorting the bald-loser.

"It must be because of her. I saw that cursed wench in the morning. She must have passed her bad luck on me!!" He started shouting and calling names to some girl he met, which piqued my curiosity.

It was highly possible the loser used his loose mouth to hurt the wench, and the girl who did this to him was the same wench. Revenge can be a dirty bitch, after all.

"Who is he talking about?" I asked Hunter, who shook his head in disbelief.

"He must've pissed the trickster. She's the Mayor's daughter who went mad two years back. Lyric Kensley. Stay away from her; she is downright crazy in her head." He explained, smirking in glee.

"As if we are any better. Look in the mirror."

"We can hold a social gathering, disparate her outcast self. People don't associate themselves with her, and whoever she finds badmouthing about her meets the same fate. Some dirty little pranks on them. Nothing harmful in the beginning, but with time, it gets plenty annoying." His words only fired my burning curiosity of the girl.

"He is right, Mr. Hotness. She is crazy. Even her doctor couldn't help." The giggle of the girl standing beside me shifted my attention. She was a nice not-my-type-bombshell.

"No thanks for the advice. I never asked for it." I went to pick a ball from the base of the net. It was safe. I saw her never reaching that far down, anyway.

Lyric. I'd like to meet-not-meet her.

Despite the excuse of a failure coach, the trials were held in swing with the other trainer. I had to borrow gym clothes from Hunter before the trials, and we began with the different height dribbles, and then simultaneously, everyone was asked to show jump hop, pro hop, and hop stop, putting the ball in the net. Later, we were divided into two small teams and played against each other. It ended just fine, and compared to my previous college teammates, these guys knew what they were doing. Yet, not enough to beat me in the game. The very game I chose because of its colour.

"Everyone played well." The assistant trainer proceeded with naming who was on the team until the end. "The captain for this team is Treyton. Anyone have an issue?"

There wouldn't be one. With a unanimous no, a loud cheer, and some pathetic cheerleading displays from the boys, the team decided to meet at one of the guy's Fraternities. They were holding a spring party. Hunter would be going too with his teammates and girlfriend, Scarlett, so I had no room to say no.

Before we could exit the hall, the loud voice from the speaker came alive. "Hello. It's an emergency. Every student must evacuate the buildings and reach the ground. I repeat, all the students are to evacuate the buildings and reach the ground. It is an emergency."

The voice went silent, and as the panic rolled in, the speaker again came to life. "This is to inform everyone... fuck yourselves. I. Am. Not. Mad!!" Soon, the water sprinklers for the fire were on, and in unison came the loud curses.

"What the fuck, she just did?!" I laughed hard.

"I told you she is lost in her head. This isn't the first time, and her father is the trustee of this University. This is the only university ready to accept that mad pianist."

That piqued more of my interest. Mayor's crazy daughter. Mad pianist.

Now, I am dying to meet that little anarchy.

CHAPTER TWO

For the past two years, the solitary life has seemed better. I had everything from a loving father to a doting brother, and memories of my dead mother fuelled me to live my dream as a pianist. I had everything until I had nothing.

I don't exist even if I am there.

"What are your plans after Masters, Grayson? Do you want to pursue a Ph.D. or like to learn the ropes of political life?" My father's newest concern is my older brother. While we both are in the same college, he is better than me. People like him, professors commend him, reporters and journalists predict his future, and many expect him to follow in my father's footsteps. He's the golden boy.

When we were kids, we decided to follow our parents. He chose Dad for his dependable and remarkable side and pursued his career in political science major in hopes of someday standing beside him and I, in love with the music my mother played and taught little kids at the community school and was known for, chose to pursue my dreams as a pianist. It was when I was five that I came across one of the hardest pieces written for piano, La Campanella.

Born with a photographic memory, it wasn't hard for me to remember the keys and the notes once I witnessed them through my eyes. Music has always been a part of me, and Mom said, she knows I am made for the music. Just like that, I became a prodigy pianist, playing one of the toughest pieces in front of the crowd at a dinner party as one of the youngest players.

My family was proud of me, and people adored me, too. Everything I cherished or thought would remain by my side didn't. Now, I have my piano and good old memories to keep me company in my chosen solitude.

I never had many friends, to begin with, but I had a social life like any other teenager. Had. Past tense. Everything dissolved in a mist.

I ruminate if my mother would be the same way my father and brother are. I am like a mole in this house, better left unattended since my presence is a nuisance.

"Did you take your pills?" Dad's sudden concern brought me out of my reverie, and I slightly nodded, ashamed that he had to be in my presence. More than the guilt of being a nuisance to him and causing him trouble, I dreaded as the time of the month approached.

Every month, on the same street, a murder happens. The very street where I first witnessed a murder and soon after was claimed as mad, who lost her sensibility because of the traumatic incident she witnessed.

I wish it ended there. It didn't. On the fifteenth of every month, even if I am locked inside a room, I'd wake up in the middle of the night on the same street with a dead body laid by my side. I witness a dead person murdering. Every time it's a different person's ghost that murders. I see the killer write on the same wall of the shop, *'Help me,'* that now stays abandoned after the first murder, where I claimed that ghosts wander and kill people.

The very word I hear from the person about to die, and then when I open my eyes, I'd be back in my room. The only difference is the news that shows pictures of the place and the murders that happened.

For the first few months after every incident, I cried and begged them to believe, only that none did. Everyone called me mad.

I tried to give an interview, and my police statements remained the same, only the victim and the murderer changing. None believed me.

Later, my father forced me to seek help, and I thought too, maybe it was something in my brain. The medicines that I was given for the said hallucinations never helped. I witness the same thing every month on the fifteenth. Nothing changed. Only my drowsiness and the rumours grow.

Wild lies that I have gone crazy.

The Mayor's crazy daughter. The mad pianist. And what not was I called. It didn't bother me at first, but when all of it started growing on people, frustrating Dad's mind, peace, and work, things took an ugly turn. My father stopped talking to me, and since then he stops by to check whether I'd taken my pills on time or not, kiss my forehead and cry assuming I'm asleep.

I take the pills. Diligently. Even if they make me a zombie in my skin, I still, for the sake of my father, do it. The pills caused hormonal imbalance, and during my periods, I go through the most painful five days of my life. I complained to my doctor about the issues, and her words, I shouldn't disappoint my father. For that very sake, I kept on taking it and went through brutal pain alone, sweating, crying, and yet couldn't ask for help. Till now, I have suffered silently.

In the pit of hell I am living in, I realised something significant. The people who ask me for help are similar to me. While they are forced to die, I am forced to be a living corpse under accusations and humiliation.

We are the same. Better dead for someone.

"You caused a nuisance again with the fire extinguishing system the prior week. Can you stop doing it every time someone speaks ill of you?" Grayson, my brother who loved me so much, too, started ignoring me when people began associating him with my problems. Eventually, those rumours and fake concerns caused my brother to lose his girlfriend he loved sincerely, and that sowed the venom of hate towards me.

"It was a prank." I tried making sense despite knowing my attempts were futile. Once, he loved me and helped me hide my fault in the pranks. It took two years to demolish the eighteen years of trust, mutual love, and respect between siblings.

"The excuse wouldn't help you, Lyric. I am already concerned for your future as it is. You've caused enough damage, so stop piling the top of the mountain." Dad reprimanded me, so I went silent again. Silently suffering, and sorry, Lyric.

Next to isolation, the only place I had was college where I could show my aggressiveness and hate for what they caused me, but now that too is becoming limited. I remember I've always been a prankster, and it was deemed childish and lovable to all despite my age.

Such a pity... the moment I became crazy for everyone, I was deemed a misfit and shunned as someone who didn't belong to any social circle.

"It's getting late; I've got a morning class." I left my food uneaten. There was a time when my father wouldn't let me leave the table before I finished my meal.

Taking my backpack, I walked out of the house. Putting my headset on, playing Mozart Piano Sonata No. 17, I sat at the back of the car as the driver pulled on the road. It was warm today, and the sun was bright in the sky. From my music to the clouds, everything danced in glee. The rhythm perfectly sank inside me and calmed my nerve-wracking mind.

When we reached, I quickly grabbed a cookie from my bag and handed it to the driver who had just joined. He smiled accepting the cookie and I walked inside the campus, making my way through the large hallways for my first lesson for vocal, then I'd be free for another three hours to practise in the music hall that no one uses because they know it belongs to me.

Maybe it didn't, but the moment the rumours spread, they stopped using it because, if anything, it had to be them who left and not the other way around. I'd fight tooth and nail to get that place to myself, and while they did show their dismay, who gives them a fuck.

"Hey, you." A masculine voice pierced my eardrums, and I was forced to take a deep breath. "Going somewhere, Chipmunk?" He whispered, his voice closer, falling heavy on my earlobes from behind, and I shivered for so many unsaid reasons.

Don't fucking sound like that.

I turned hastily. My face suddenly blank with annoyance, painting my features. He's the new guy I fucked up with the previous week. While walking in the empty halls, I saw him fucking one of my classmates in the music room. The sacred place in the entire world, and my beloved piano was forced to watch them fucking. That's blasphemy. Their moans sounded like two people who needed oxygen masks at all costs to keep them alive.

What would that result in?

Everyone knows. I went to him while he was having lunch in the on-campus cafeteria, and in the loudest voice, told him, "I am sorry. I poked holes in your condom yesterday when you were practising in the court." He paled, hearing me, and his friend, the captain guy from football, glared at me as if he would pummel me to death for my art work.

This captain guy from basketball started shouting when the girl he fucked came there, and upon hearing, she instantly assured him she was on pills.

I fucked with her, too, because I told her I changed her pills a week before with vitamins in the music room. They both went pale, and started shouting and cursing, but I fled from the scene of the crime, and both of them didn't come to the college as I heard the prior week until this Monday.

Treyton, as I've come to know his name, came to me soon upon his return and dragged me from my historical music lecture in front of the professor, but wasn't scolded because his famous friend was backing him up, to a silent hall and blasted. He told me he knew I never swapped that girl's pills, and whatever, she wasn't pregnant either.

I confessed with my sweet, innocent face that I never did poke holes or swapped pills. I just pranked him and technically lied to him with my words.

Speechless, he stormed away.

Worse happened when he pranked me by distributing my phone number with a witch's picture on pamphlets to the entire college the next day that said, *'Contact if you want to know your future.'* And I spent two days telling people why they can't get girlfriends or why are they still virgins, or even the horny arse guys and girls wanting to have phone sex. I changed my number yesterday.

"I never allowed you to use nicknames with me." I grumbled, crossing my hands over my breasts, and he watched me silently until his gaze made me uncross my hands, to his very delight.

Oh, I knew he's a pervert. How scandalous.

"Chipmunk, that's not for you to decide. So, how are you going to retaliate?" His huge grin tickled my belly unexpectedly.

Chewing my lips, I huffed a breath and shared a thin smile in response.

"You'll find your answer when the next girl you fuck accidentally gets pregnant." I squinted my eyes, about to turn and leave, but he grabbed me by my shoulder and leaned close to my face, his lips brushing my ear.

"Would it be you?"

"In your fucking nightmares. Don't force me to make you impotent."

His laugh was musical, and here until a week before, I thought he needed oxygen masks. Interesting.

"What is happening here?" A deep, ominous voice slithered up my spine, sending chills through me for every conceivable wrong reason.

I recoiled from Treyton as my brother's face appeared behind him. He moved too, hearing the man, and looked between us. Treyton said nothing despite my brother throwing glares at him.

"Gray-"

"You were supposed to be in class, weren't you?" Grayson barked, and the entire buzzing hall went silent. It was their golden boy who was angry. How'd they not respect it with their shut mouths?!

"I was, Gray. I am heading there."

Without anything further exchanged, he side stepped Treyton, grabbed my arm, and hauled me through the corridor. I silently followed, saying nothing much.

While walking away, I looked over my shoulder, watching Treyton bloody pissed while his best friend was calming him as he put his hand in his pocket and cursed, looking at me with slime stuck to his lighter in hand and sticking my tongue out, I smiled.

He murmured, and I saw his lips curving in a beautiful feral grin.

Suddenly, I anticipated his answer to my actions.

"Look in front."

I instinctively dropped my head in surrender, my eyes glued to the ground as we approached the intersection of the hall.

"Stay away from that guy. He's not good, and neither is his friend, who is even worse. Do you get it? Treyton Spade is the deputy commissioner's son, and we don't know what those guys would do for your madness, and for all I know, once the fifteenth arrives in three days, they'd come knocking on the doors of our home. Before they choose you as their scapegoat, fucking get to your senses and act accordingly. You represent the Mayor as his daughter; if anything, you must think of our father." He chided, and I kept listening to him until we reached my class.

"Goodbye," I was about to enter and be away from him, the least I wanted.

"Wait, you forgot your pills on your desk. Take them now." He placed the tablet in my hand and waited for me to consume that hideous pill.

It'd turn me into a zombie.

Knowing I had no room to argue, I forced the pill into my mouth, chewed aggressively, and swallowed without water.

"Can I go?" There was contempt in my voice.

Breathing deeply, he nodded, taking his leave. I went to my seat in the far back where no one would be bothered nor would bother me.

It is going to be hard. I tried avoiding the pills and instead took a headache medicine for today and promised myself I'd take them in the evening.

Welcome to the zombie apocalypse.

CHAPTER THREE

"I promise, this has to be the most hilarious of all." Hunter laughed, pushing me inside the cafeteria, where his girlfriend Scarlett came rushing in before stealing my whore from me. As he walked away with her, I couldn't fathom how that devil fell for an angel. Though I've got nothing against it. She is his only family alive who cares for him genuinely.

Spotting me alone, some of my teammates in the corner with the cheerleading group called me to join. I don't like to hang around anyone other than Hunter, and I had no interest because the focus of my attention was robbed, and perjury was done by none other than the Chipmunk, who was sitting quietly in the corner with a plate of burger and fries.

I sat across from her, trying to gouge out a response because I returned the slime favour with a condom filled with my cum in her locker. She must be pissed after that, and I'd love to see what next she comes up with.

I waited for straight ten minutes. She didn't respond and

kept nibbling on her burger, just like a Chipmunk. However, the behaviour she showed seemed peculiar. While I know about the tittle-tattles, I've considered hearing her side before deciding to claim her as mad or not. My father's job has rubbed on me to some extent. It is to reason. And taking a practical and grounded approach.

I've collected enough information. People's mean words must hurt, but she serves those verbal abuses with the cold revenge dish that draws my conclusion with enough proof that she isn't being bullied actively through actions, which may be because she's the Mayor's daughter.

"Chipmunk," I called her, having enough of the silent treatment.

She didn't hear me or pretended not to until I knocked on the end of her side of the table. She finally looked up.

Fuck.

Her eyes were dead. She stared at me for a long time before shaking her head vigorously, and I could see how her actions raised concerns for others who looked at her scared. As if that didn't short-circuit my mind, she started banging her head on the table screaming, and for a second there, I was shocked.

"Captain, you should move away, we don't know what that crazy bitch will do. Don't associate yourself with her." One of my teammates yelled over the top of Lyric's scream. That warning destroyed my composure, and I hated that he decided to use words that didn't appeal to me in the least about a girl, who I hate because she is a little anarchy who loves pranking and nearly fucked me up with the thought of becoming a father at my age.

Whispers surrounded the room, and some panicked were asking each other to go and call for a staff member to come, but before any of that could happen, I moved quickly. Scooping her body in my arms, I rushed out of there.

I was not sure where to take her. For some reason, my intuition said that the infirmary wasn't an option. I knew that the piano room that she occupied always remained empty. With that in mind, I moved quickly. Her entire face was hidden behind the curtain of her arse long copper blonde hair, and her tiny strawberry-shaped body that fitted perfectly in my arms trembled as she repeatedly banged her head on my shoulder.

I entered the room and laid her on the sofa, locking the doors before coming back to her. She went silent. Her eyes were closed, hiding the alluring chestnut browns filled with so much mystery.

"I am sorry," she whispered, her eyes still closed. I sat on the coffee table, observing her.

"What are you sorry for, Chipmunk?" I had to clasp my hands together, reading back my memory in the cafeteria. How they all treated her like she wasn't a person. None even came to help her and had the time of the day to warn me. It could've been a fucking seizure, but those bloody rascals are all the same porcupines in a rotten forest.

Seeing red haze like this wasn't supposed to sound good, but fucking up with those bastards did appeal to me.

Brushing the curls from her face, I don't know why I caressed her cheeks. Her face was red, and her bright, warm ivory skin paled as she curled into a ball. Her timidness at the moment spiked the memory from the morning and how her brother treated her. If not for Hunter signalling me through his eyes to retreat, I wouldn't have suppressed the deep burning red consuming me and the desire to burn that man surging in the marrow of my bone. And to say she put slime on my lighter was not the best move.

At that moment, Hunter somehow brought me to the back of the college ground, away from the crowd, and tossed me a borrowed lighter. It was a lost sperm in a race compared to my lighter, Lyric destroyed. Even her fucking name is too sweet to be hers.

I still found some peace by burning the wood chips and leaves. *Yay,' a great campfire.* Not.

I'm still pissed. Her condition isn't helping me either.

"I embarrassed you there, didn't I?" She whispered, sounding loathsome, and the blame was on her in her tone.

"You did not, Chipmunk. Why do you think this would embarrass me over the stunt you pulled with the condom and contraceptives? I should've just asked you the flavour at that time, but I lost my screws hearing you. So, tell me, what happened?" I waited again, patiently. At the very least, I can act as one.

Her tired chuckle resonated before she spoke. "Nothing.

You've earned nothing to be answered."

"It's not very wise to say when I could kill you here and flee. In the end, people would consider you attempted suicide from craziness." My words came out more hotly than it should've been. I regretted none.

"Very brave of you. Let me rest, and don't you dare make a sound. And the head banging was my way of getting back at out. Now, people are going to fuck up with your social life. Thank me later." Another tired chuckle before a little snore filled the air.

If she was a man, I would've dragged her by the hair and turned her into a pulp of blood and organs. Bloody little Chipmunk. This little anarchy won't stop at anything, and if she thinks people ignoring me would mean anything, then she lost this round. I fucking care not what they believe in the first place. However, she speaks about humiliating me. I don't think she would've done that. At any cost, it just proved to the onlookers she is crazy in her head.

I kept staring at her. It all started with a curiosity that turned into a back-and-forth battle of treachery. It keeps things heated and fun for me. Yet, I want more. This much doesn't satisfy me. I want to know more about her mystery. It bothers me how bearing so much, she keeps a straight face. Since the moment I've known her, and what even Scarlett and Hunter told me of, they never have seen her crying over the abuse and humiliation.

I kept looking at her, ignoring multiple texts and calls from Hunter.

Lyric. I want to know you more.

What happened today keeps bothering me. I know Lyric Kensley has been a certified mental patient. As for my thoughts, I don't think she is, and this means I'd be consulting my psychologist in secrecy. Something I hate to do.

Light footsteps tapping the floorboard closed. There was a

rhythm to that monotonous voice and the calming smell of lavender that embraced me and filled the needed tranquillity. The thoughts that bother me humble in her presence.

"What's bothering my boy?" Mom ruffled my hair, her light golden blonde locks open, but unlike hers, I have more on the curlier side. It isn't like chihuahua or afro, but curly and hard to maintain. Yet, I liked the idea of resembling my mother's attributes more, be it hair colour or eyes and skin tone, and I am good with one thing not matching. Our heights. For that gene code, my father can take the credit.

"Something is bothering me." I sat by the window bed, looking into the night with crickets buzzing at the arrival of spring.

"Is it a girl problem, finally?" She sat on my bed, blinking stars.

I shook my head, not even bothering to clear it. "Have you heard of Lyric Kensley?"

"That gifted pianist?"

It took me by surprise. I've heard all kinds of names over the past two weeks since I joined St. Evelyn University, but it's the first time something about that Chipmunk doesn't have some humiliation attached.

"Yes. How do you know her?" That fucking curiosity about that girl, the interest that devours me from inside. I want to know everything about her to the very bits and pieces, so the little anarchy could hide nothing and never outsmart me again.

"She has a recital every Sunday in the community hall. I know, it must be the gossip you heard in your college, despite that, people come and attend all of it. Be it a concert or any musical for charity, she is a young star in the field and is treated so. I heard her music, and it's soulful. The moment her fingers caress the keys, she becomes one with the notes and produces the most melodic harmony. I'd say you should join me this Sunday. You'd love to hear," she suggested, and I dropped the topic with a vague nod. My mother never asked or required me to tell her more. She knows I'll deal with it in my way or highway.

She has become accustomed to disaster management.

"Also, now that you asked, it reminds me about an envelope your father just received. It's from Lyric Kensley. The name of the receiver wasn't mentioned so... he took it to his study."

There are times in life when you want to question your

existence and if not, there are others enough to make that instance possible. In my life, Lyric Kensley has taken over that prominent figure's form.

"Fuck! Mom, you should've told me sooner. Run!!" I shouted, sprinting in the air, jumping over my bed, and running out of my room, cursing and speeding through the hall. For the first time, I'm glad I am a sportsman.

Picking up speed, I skipped the stairs, took the right turn, and banged open the second door, looking at my dad reading a document in hand.

I breathed in relief.

"Dad, the envelope you received is for-"

"You?" He looked at me from the papers with a critical eye gesture.

"Yes," I admitted, walking inside and about to look for the paper before finding my way out.

"Good to hear, so you can explain to me what these papers are about and why did you whore yourself?" He growled, throwing the papers on his desk and pushing his hair backwards.

Dumbfounded, I walked closer and picked up the papers, sensing my mother's steps behind me as she entered the room.

AGREEMENT

This business agreement is made between **Lyric Harmony Kensley** (Party A) and **Treyton Cadwell Spade** (Party B). The tenure of this agreement is from 03/13/XX28 (MM/DD/YYYY) to 12/13/XX29 (MM/DD/YYYY). None of the parties can withdraw from the business services before the completion of tenure. In case of violation of the contract from either of the parties, they shall be charged with the penalty of going naked in public and enacting monkey, dog, cat, and elephant before signing themselves into slavery to the wronged party. Also, in case of mutual agreement to terminate the contract, each party is responsible for paying each other with their nudes.

Personal Details (Party A)

Name: Lyric Harmony Kensley
Address: XXX Knightsbridge, London
Contact No.: XXXXXX9071

Personal Details (Party B)
Name: Treyton Cadwell Spade
Address: XXX Greenwich, London
Contact No.: XXXXXX4445

Party A and Party B must adhere to the following clauses stated below. In case of failing to meet the stated clauses, the mentioned party wronged in the phrased case shall refer to the mentioned penalty on the previous page.

The clauses of the agreement are stated below:

Clause A. Party B will satisfy all the sexual needs of Party A only when consented and using safe words, i.e. a word previously agreed upon for use as a signal during sex, especially sex involving bondage, dominance, or sadism, to let the other party know that they should stop what they are doing.

Clause B. Party A shall be in the role of 'Master/Dominant', and Party B shall be in the role of 'Slave/Submissive' for any sexual interaction or intercourse that would occur between the two parties. Party A, the dominant, and Party B, the submissive dynamic, is a top/bottom dynamic. While Party A, the dominant partner or top, is the one taking control in spanking, bonding, whipping, or other sexual scenarios, Party B, the submissive or bottom, may also keep control by demanding the top perform certain roles or insist on switching.

Clause C. Under specified circumstances by Party A shall Party A and Party B be allowed to switch i.e. the involved parties may shift between the dominant and submissive roles, depending on Party A and the context.

Clause D. Party B shall only be involved in the following sexual interactions apart from intercourse with Party A.

1. *Bondage.* The state or practice of being physically restrained, such as by being tied up, chained, or put in handcuffs

for sexual gratification.

2. *Pyrophilia.* Usage of fire and wax to cause mild burns such as heat sensation and redness on skin for sexual gratification.

3. *Foreplay.* It can include a lot of different things, like kissing, sharing fantasies, or touching one another's genitals, such as fingering, etc. The purpose of foreplay is to add to sexual excitement.

4. *Roleplay.* An activity in which consenting partners assume the roles of different characters in an imaginary scenario during sex.

5. *Anal sex.* Penetration of anal for sexual pleasure.

6. *Oral sex.* Using your mouth, lips, or tongue to stimulate your partner's genitals or anus. Such as 'blow job,' '69,' 'rimming,' etc.

7. *Fisting.* To insert the hand into the rectum or vagina of (someone) as a means of sexual stimulation.

8. *Spanking.* The act of hitting with the hand, usually several times on the bottom, as a punishment or for sexual pleasure.

9. *Hair pulling.* It involves frequent or repeated actions to pull out hair from a partner's scalp, which can increase the intensity and emotional connection during sex. It can also be a way to assert dominance or submission, depending on the dynamic of the relationship.

10. *Blindfolding.* A piece of cloth tied around the head to cover your partner's eyes to enhance the remaining senses, focusing attention on sound, smells, and physical contact. This increased awareness is said to allow for greater excitement and anticipation by eliminating visual cues, for the partner who cannot see what to expect.

11. *Whipping.* The use of a whip means that the dominant must take great care to hit the intended target area and avoid wrapping; when a whip or flogger makes contact with the target area somewhere up its length and the remaining length wraps around the submissive's body to deliver a sharp, erotic, and possibly non-injurious off-target blow to excite in form of a sexual punishment or reward as per the dynamic in the relationship.

12. *Choking.* Having a partner's hands, or an object, on or around their neck or having their hands on or around their

partner's neck during sex or a situation for sexual pleasure or to excite a partner sexually.

Clause E. Party A shall take care of every financial or monetary need of Party B.

Clause F. Rules that must be established to conduct behaviour, relationship presentation or dynamic in close intimacy, or public appearance as a couple must be as follows:

RULES

1. Whenever Party A and Party B are in a public setup, whatever the place it shall be, Party B will bow to Party A.
2. Party B shall address Party A as 'Master' regardless of place or situation until stated otherwise by Party A.
3. Party B must show gratitude for every punishment given as much as for reward.
4. In every sexual setup, Party B must address in a specific elaborate explanation discussing their need, wants, and desires, followed by a 'Please' to Party A.
5. Party B will wear any given gift or present or any form of reward and punishment with pride and gratitude, displaying Party A's claim and ownership of Party B in public and private.
6. Party B shall never bow, or submit to anyone else other than Party A. Party B must always keep their head straight, maintain eye contact, and present themselves with great emphasis as they carry the claim of Party A and represent them.
7. Party B shall reply to every asked question or statement to Party A without hesitation, burden, or thought as Party A has all the right to interfere in Party B's life, share their problems, burdens and assist them in every situation, and vice versa shall stand true for both the party under rule no. 6 and rule no.7.
8. Party B shall kiss Party A every time they meet.
9. Party B should be accustomed to being called baby boy by his sugar mommy, who is Party A here.
10. Party B must take Party A on two romantic dates every week.
11. BDSM and sexual intercourse aftercare must involve kissing, cuddling, hydrating, bathing together, listening to music, watching games and movies, sleeping next to each other,

cooking, and communicating from Party B to Party A.

The amount to be paid to Party B from Party A for the sugar mommy Lyric's baby boy Treyton agreement is 1000000/- GBP only. In words, One Million Pounds Sterling only.

Lyric signed the contract in the end, and I looked up at my father, who cocked his brow at me. My mouth was hanging open, and it was nothing compared to the migraine that suddenly hammered my skull.

"How the fuck she comes up with these? I would love to know." I pinched between my eyes.

"And to think, my one and only son becomes someone's sugar baby. What an achievement?" Dad clapped, and Mom looked at me amused.

"Dad," I growled in warning, but his clapping didn't stop.

"At least you proved me wrong because I thought that you'd come home with your sugar baby, so there is an improvement." He made the snide remark again, and red flared vibrantly in front of my eyes.

Oh, Chipmunk, pray that you'd never come in front of me again.

Before Mom could join Dad, the phone in my pants started vibrating. Given the circumstances, I wanted to ignore it, but the vibration won't stop. Bringing my phone out of my pocket, I glared at the screen as it flashed an unknown number, but for some reason, I knew who it was.

"Young man, on speakers." My father glared, and I was compelled to oblige. Attending the call on speaker, I addressed the person.

"Treyton Spade, speaking. Who am I talking to?" My tone was pissed.

"Hey, baby boy. Did you receive my gift?" The glee in the voice forced me to pinch the bridge of my nose as I placed the paper and the phone on Dad's table and brought my lighter out, rotating the spark wheel as the fire burned and extinguished.

"Should I be happy you're paying me one million or worried you have my details downright accurate?" There was a subtle amusement in my tone hearing her voice, and my hands vigorously played with the spark wheel.

"Oh, come on, Treyton. I'm the Mayor's daughter. Getting your information is as easy as buying skin care products online."

This fucking woman!

"Chipmunk, a piece of news. Your delivery man sent the package in the wrong hands."

She went silent. Completely silent, and I nearly mistook it that she ended the call. Nearly is the keyword.

"And... Who..." She trailed, scared.

"My father, David Spade, received the contract and is currently listening to our conversation." I informed, smirking because she went silent again.

"Hello, Mr. Spade," her meek voice resonated, addressing Dad who looked at me from the phone. His eyes glistened with a mysterious shine.

"Hello, young lady. I never knew you had such exotic sexual preferences," he remarked, smirking.

"I never knew, too." Her voice faltered again, and Dad had to bite his knuckles to stop laughing out loud. Mom, on the other hand, kept hearing the exchange with the same mysterious shine that my father had.

"So, for having my father call me sugar baby and a whore, what should I give in return for this prank, Ms. Kensely?" I asked. The urge to see her was borderline psychotic at this instance. What kind of face would she be making? The unknown wilderness in her chestnut eyes, I want to know.

Fuck. I want to commit every one of the sins she has enlisted on that piece of paper.

"Should I send your father my dick pics, would that be sufficient, sugar mommy?" The tease in my voice, even I could smell the lingering scent of addictiveness in me.

"Not a great choice. My father is an arse man, I think, so pull your pants down in front of a floor-length mirror, turn around and take a mirror selfie of your arse and send it with heart emojis. I promise he'd love to see it. And you can share the dick pics with my brother. Most welcome from their side, baby boy. Good night." Saying so, she immediately disconnected, and my father and mother burst into hysterical laughter.

I couldn't say; I wasn't grinning, and she was by far the most embarrassed, and her tone filled in the gaps of her reaction I wanted to witness.

"Lavender, I'd love to speak to her in person, but guess I cannot. Fifteenth is around the corner, and things would get ugly." My father's words drew lines on my forehead.

Yes, I know about the serial murder case and Chipmunk's involvement. I, too, know just as much currently as my father does from the case files he has. We talk over dinner, and he only shares his thoughts, not the confidential information. It's on me, who hides in the dark of the night and breaks into his office to fuel my burning curiosity.

Lyric Kensely sees dead people's ghosts on the fifteenth of every month, murdering people on the same street and writing 'Help me' from the victim's blood on the shop's wall. The only difference is not the pattern of murder since every victim dies with multiple knife stabs. The difference is the identity of the victim and the murderer.

A human's ghost. A new victim of high society.

CHAPTER FOUR

When you can feel your shadow following you everywhere, it signifies your mental state, and mine isn't great to begin with, and on several occasions, it causes a nuisance to human society.

I watch every step I take. I look around myself. I observe people. I find corners to escape. Since, it's the fourteenth of the month today, and tonight, when the darkness of the fifteenth would fall, shall my doom flag would do too.

"What are you looking at?" Ignoring Grayson, I draw the curtains of my room and go back to the bed. Skipping college isn't new. I know when to step back from the flooding voices of watchful eyes and draw a line. I've trained myself in these two years and after twenty-seven murders.

A big number of deaths.

Why couldn't the police still find the perpetrators?

I question myself daily: What was my fault that I am standing here?

Initially, I thought my brother would help me if not someone else, and the only answer that I ever received from Grayson after repeating countless times the same question that I ask myself, "I speak to you no differently than I ever have, Lyric. I wouldn't find fault with others if I were you. That you shouldn't blame others for what you're going through. Is it that hard to understand?"

And like the doting sister I've always been, who looks up to her brother despite the harsh way he treats her, I'll reply monotonously, 'It's not, brother. Sorry for troubling you.' Then I'll turn and walk away.

I never came to understand what was so hard. To be neglected by my father out of thin air or to be hated by my brother who'd once do anything for me?

I wish to understand my life and myself.

"Will you be attending the community hall recital today?" He inquired and I looked at my phone kept on the nightstand. The thought of overstepping my drawn boundaries haunted me. I couldn't force myself to pick up my phone and reply to Treyton who'd been messaging me since yesterday, asking my whereabouts. I don't get why he cares if I am in college or not as if we're friends.

The most I know of our current relationship is we're borderline enemies, at least what I find fitting for our exchange. But his advances unnerve me. Enemies are not supposed to keep continuous tabs like this and be concerned for each other. I am not, but his texts speak differently to me, and maybe he is the only person who dared check on me. The only number in my phone, apart from the six listed numbers, calls me, texts me, and shows enough interest to know *how I'm doing.*

"It's not Sunday," I reminded him, looking at my feet. I want to paint my nails. Don't know when was the last time, I went to buy something out of pure self-love in these two years. What about doing my hair, and maybe adding some highlights and shopping for a dress and hairpin?

Do I have the money for it? The very thing I remember is my own earned money resting untouched in my bank account, whose authority lies in my brother's hand. Because I am not medically stable for anyone to believe me, I can hold accountability for my things.

If I get a chance today, will I be allowed to go and buy a

coffee for myself? I heard some girls the other day talking about this eatery near our college. They said they serve some delicious meals. I wish I could go, but I know Dad and Grayson wouldn't allow it.

For my pills to work, I am supposed to have a certain type of meal prescribed by the doctor and should take my pills on time.

However, the idea of escaping just once does sound great. I wonder, how much money does one need to travel from a cab or public transport? What would be the price for a cup of coffee? How much do I have spend to at least buy a drink cheap enough to fit my budget?

"I'd suggest you check your schedule for once. Today, you promised the dean of the music department a charity recital." He implored, and I groaned instantly, remembering my promise to him.

Christopher Danbury, my professor, might be the only person among the staff who doesn't give me a side-eye.

Although he once tried talking me into telling him about my nights of the fifteenth with pure intentions of helping me out.

Sadly, upon hearing this, Uncle Henry, who assists my father got angry and warned him. I was afraid he might force Professor Danbury to quit his job, so I started keeping my distance. Only ever indulging him into talks about music and studies. The more minimal the interaction, the better.

Uncle Henry advised me never to speak of the hallucinations, as it might jeopardize my father's and brother's future. Despite how we're living, I love my family, so I decided to shut up and never speak about myself to anyone in existence.

"I'll be attending it. I won't break my promise whatsoever." With a snide remark and a mean girl look, I hasten to change my pj's and slippers into jeans, bat sleeves shirt, and vans. My hair in a tight pony and a baseball cap partially to hide my face brought together my look.

As I grabbed my backpack to head out, Grayson stopped me midway. I didn't glance at him, as I stood by the door while he was still inside my room.

"I never broke my promise to you, Lyric." His assertive voice doesn't melt my heart anymore.

True, that I love him. He is my brother. That's something no one can take away from me, neither his ex nor he can do. I just hope he knew what it meant to be Lyric Kensely for once.

"Yes. You've never been wrong, brother. You never broke any promise to me because you never made one to me." I poked the inside of my cheek with my tongue and gulped a heavy lump down my throat.

I do not cry easily, but that doesn't mean I do not hurt.

Right now, I feel as if my chest has been ripped open, and it hurts like a bitch.

Walking away from him, my steps somehow dragged themselves to the waiting car outside the gates in the driveway of the mansion. While, I pondered on my commendable act of victory. This might be the first time in years that I spoke so rudely to Grayson.

I guess it started when he stopped calling me baby sister and annihilated the loving brother image in my eyes. The moment he became a brother to me from old-Gray-person.

Sitting in the back of the car, I watched my surroundings blur into a single color. It wasn't until the driver's voice broke through my zoned-out moment that I realized we had arrived.

"Should I expect to pick you up?"

I nodded, while giving him a cookie from my bag. Once he passed a small smile, accepting the sweet treat, I turned around, skipping up the steps to the community hall for the charity recital, and rushed inside.

Halfway through, making my way inside the building, I met Professor Danbury, who escorted me to a dressing room where I changed into a plain ivory satin dress, and a pair of black heels, setting my arse long hair into a bun and walking to the backstage of the auditorium.

I kept telling myself in the passing momentum of my actions, someday it would eventually hurt less. Someone would eventually trust you for your lies. Someone would eventually cherish you despite your flaws. Just wait for that someone, and make a promise to yourself not to give up until that someone arrives.

I already know there is no such thing as a perfect timing, but even in the wrong if my someone decides to appear, I wish to recognize before it's too late. Although, I don't know what to do if my someone is wrong and not the situation.

When my name was called, I walked to sit behind the vintage piano. The soft glow enveloping me, the misty haze created by the artificial simulators covering the expanse, and the obscurity lulled my burning heart to a numb sleep.

Closing my eyes and remembering my mother smiling at me as she sang and played an old tune on her piano, I started writing my feelings in the tone of my notes before opening my eyes and strumming the keys with a heated passion. This piece was my original. It's been long since I created something new.

This piece also have a major flaw that doesn't come off as appealing to me as to everyone else apart from Grayson and my teacher.

This piece is empty just like my days. It doesn't have a sorrow to cry for or a rhythm to smile at, nor does it make oneself anxious to fall in love or beg in despair. It's just that, it's empty, just like me because this is the music I created when I didn't know who to speak to.

I hope someday my hollowness will be filled with something and I can sincerely apologise to music and return the seeking with a wisdom of my own and not borrowed from memories or my gift.

As the musical serendipity came to its gorgeous end, I gathered the courage to look into the eyes of my audience with hesitation, dread hidden under pursuit of the shadow of every reflection I met.

Lights illuminated the hall, and everyone stood up from their seats, thundering with a unanimous clapping sound.

There was appreciation in their eyes. A serene look dominated each one of them, and then came the most beautiful pair of orbs, paralysing me. Whiskeys bearing an aggressive look and questions only I could answer.

The exchange between our orbs lasted for a few seconds. He sipped the wine in hand and talked to a beautiful lady in a classy lavender dress holding his hand. She was a proper woman of high society, which many magazines feature and like to portray. Her small face was adorned with stray locks, and her big, warm, and gentle whiskey eyes were filled with love as she looked at him. Despite her elegant features, I could still spot the similarity between them.

His harsh, rough, and rugged features, boasting masculinity in a delicious formal suit, did hold some similarities to the petite woman.

While Treyton had light golden blonde locks that were short and wavy but styled to perfection like his narcissistic self, she had straight ones tied in an elegant braid.

While he stood at a height of 6'3 with muscles gorgeously shaping him, she was on the average height of 5'6, and compared to her, I was tiny at 5'3. At least one would love to slide their hands around her waist, unlike me, who couldn't even make her crush fall for her, but overall, the similarities and differences never ended there for them because both had a beautiful brandy tan complexion, and it was impossible to not be addicted to this destruction they carried in their ambience.

If for no other reason, it was sufficient to turn heads towards the pair. Treyton always kept a clean shaved look that appealed to his attractiveness and made him stand out in the crowd. I don't know why or how, but it's been some time since I started noticing him in a different light.

As Professor Danbury brought the crowd's attention to him, taking over the stage from me, I did a pretty princess courtesy and took my leave.

In the back, I changed into my clothes and grabbed my backpack, ready to leave. Not bothering to wait until the end for the meet and greet and the thank you flower ceremony.

The highlights of occasions turn dim if I am there. I know when to understand where I am not welcome. My participation check would be deposited in my bank, and Grayson would take my permitted action and donate it to the charity my mother created for disabled children's education. At least one thing happens on my accord.

Breathing deep, I step into the evening air. The sun would set in nearly two hours, and I'd be home alone, cooped in my blanket and dreading the tick-tock of my clock.

"I thought way too highly of you, didn't I, Chipmunk?" The voice that shouldn't be echoing in this world, or mine, danced like music to my ears. I took a deep breath and slowly turned, staring at him.

He looked beautiful, and so damn everything I know could never belong to me. The madness I sleep with ruins people and pushes them away from me.

"Hello, Treyton. Good to see you here." I waved, fixing the backpack on my shoulder and avoiding his gaze.

One step.

He took the forbidden step towards me, and I bit my bottom lip.

Two steps.

Why was he coming near?

Three steps.

Oh no, I don't know what to say to him.

Four steps.

Stop there.

Why was he getting close to me?

"Look at me." His gruff voice commanded, and I took another desperate breath, meeting his addictive eyes.

He stood close. Way too close.

He overpowered me with his dominating height and irresistible presence.

He removed my baseball cap, carving my face in his addictive eyes.

"Now, I can see the real anarchy." He smirked. His gaze touched me in a way I had never been touched before, and never would have without him.

His fingers gently grazed my cheeks, tickling the skin that burned under his touch. Those intense eyes locked with my chestnut ones, silently begging me to say something, anything, as long as it speaks to him.

"Did you like my performance?" I was taken off guard by my words. Never in my entire life have I ever sought after someone's approval. Not even my family or teacher. Yet, suddenly, his previous words knocked at a dark corner of my heart and gauged deeper.

"It was hollow, Chipmunk. I heard your music is soulful, but all it resonated was notes of emptiness rattling in a cage. I may haven't heard your song before, but I know it wasn't you there, and I fucking want you. I want the real you in the rhythm that makes me lose my consciousness over a damn music with no words but deeper meanings." The rumbling growl, low in octave, challenged me.

Why?

Why was he doing that?

Why does he want me, the girl shunned by everyone?

"Treyton, please..." I begged, looking deep into his eyes with glittering tears. I want to feel the freedom. I want to be me for once.

I want to buy a coffee for myself. I want to buy a dress. I want to do my hair like other girls do. I want to paint my nails. I want to eat outside for once and not the meals and pills they feed me. For once, I want to be Lyric in my music.

"Chipmunk, what happened?" He questioned. Concern drawn on his handsome face.

"Can you take me out of here? I want to do things. I want to eat out. Buy a dress. Can you take me shopping, please? I promise I'll return your money–"

"Chipmunk, calm down. Shhh..." He hushed, pulling me close, circling my waist in his strong arms as if promising me the protection I craved.

His forehead dropped on mine. It was a silent peace, and I'd have never thought of being so close to someone I barely know, but sometimes, wrong choices become the only choice one can have, and I chose him.

"You don't have to worry about some fucking pounds. Let me take you out, my sugar mommy? The contract said so, two dates per week, at the very least." He grinned. The glee in his eyes sparkled, and I nodded immediately.

"Yes, baby boy," I confidently claimed his embrace when he put some distance between us and interlaced his hand with mine.

"Let me show you what my kind of paradise looks like, Chipmunk?"

I know it's not like my hell.

CHAPTER FIVE

I never knew wind could feel so good on one's skin. I also never knew Treyton, who stood as the definition of society's elegant boy in front of me this afternoon, would be a biker. Yet, bikers in suits do look pretty hot.

Holding him tight and pressing my breasts on his back, I inhaled. The inside of the helmet messed up my hair, and the scent that lingered in it did something to my head.

I was feeling bold—desperate even. So, I did what I'd never do in a million lifetimes. Running my hands gently over his front, I hesitated at first, but when he picked up speed, I held on to him tighter, my heart racing—feeling bold, so bold. I groped his pec and squeezed hard. The reaction was so amazing that he took an emergency break by the curb and turned fast to look at me, risking a whiplash.

I couldn't see his face through the helmet but the elapsing moment turned me into a giddy mess, and giggles rushed through my lips.

"Does that sound like a joke to you, Chipmunk?" Was he

angry? I couldn't tell, but I couldn't stop laughing either.

"I am so sorry." I laughed hard.

"What was that for?" Why was he being so fussy about it, as if I assaulted him?

Oh, maybe I did.

The realisation of my joke not coming out as just a joke slaughtered my smile. I instantly felt bad and apologetic for what I did.

Removing my helmet, I waited for him. Once he removed his helmet and put the stand out, killing the engine, I faced him. He stood beside me while I was still seated in my position on the bike, guilt playing the pathetic role.

"I am really sorry. I just thought it might shock you, and the expectation of your reaction being a whole lot of fun triggered me to do so. I never realised until it happened that touching without permission could be demeaning to you, too." My eyes, bearing his addictive ones, implored for forgiveness.

He cleared his throat, shifting from one foot to the other for some reason.

"That calls for compensation, isn't it?" The rough voice of his overbearing self and the arrogant smirk told me how much he wasn't the least bit bothered by what I did, yet, I did something that sounded offensive to me, so I was ready to bear the price.

"What do you need? I'll do anything you'd ask me to." I already regretted my words. Was I falling for a devil's trap?

"Anything?" He leaned closer. Our faces were inches apart. I could feel his breath, the sharp contour of his face perfectly carving his hotness, and the way his eyes were shifting between my eyes and parted lips bothered me. Not to forget his damn voice. Why does he speak in that sexy voice that does something inside my stomach?

That sexy voice, that sounded like he cared.

"A-Any-thing." I stuttered, and the ego boost he got from my loser self was massive.

"Don't forget, I'll be using my golden ticket soon," he warned, winked, and grabbed the helmet from my hand, putting it back on my head and fastening the lock before doing his and returning the bike on the busy London road.

I was observing his reflection in the side mirror the whole

ride. Once we reached the mall, he parked, and hand in hand, we walked inside.

"Let's begin with your list. What do you want to do first?" He asked, stepping beside me in the elevator.

"I want to do my hair and paint my nails. Then, I want to buy a red dress and a matching hair ribbon. Then, a movie, a coffee, and dinner in a fancy place." I never thought I'd be saying all this loud, and someone would be listening to me to fulfil it. Absurd.

"Sounds like a lot."

Again, the guilt came. Treyton doesn't have to be the one doing so. We weren't even friends to begin with, and yes, I said I'd return the money, but how was I supposed to, when I couldn't even bring myself to ask my father or brother for help?

"I am sorry." I apologised, stepping out of the elevator with him.

"You're apologising a lot unnecessarily today, and for the fact, you don't even have to. I said I don't fucking care about some pounds." He emphasised.

"That doesn't mean, it is a non-existent value. You're giving me money, and I feel guilty because you're not obliged to be here with me. We're not friends and you're going out of your way to fulfil my wishes."

"If your self-pity party is over, I'd like to get things done because all I have with you is this evening to live. To get to be with the girl who keeps me on my toes and gets a free pass every time she does something awful, for which I would've burned her alive if she was someone else. And I promise you, Chipmunk, with me, you're safe to express, which may not come free, but for you, it comes as an exception. You don't need a label to be mine or be with me. You just have to focus and anchor us in whichever direction you want us to go, and I'll go. I'll follow your lead." He smiled, the most sadistic one that could exist, and despite the burning image, I loved it.

With Treyton, being myself became natural. We hit it off the moment we met, and however we are as a person, it doesn't matter how short it's been since we have known each other because, for some reason, I feel so strongly about us that it's an absurdity to think fate doesn't exist.

For all I care, I could say, we've known each other our entire lives without ever meeting. With the kind of communication I have with him, I don't think I could ever hide anything or have a misunderstanding when he's around.

When he is involved, everything becomes music. My life becomes easy and I could play through it without feeling the need to hide.

It scares me how his words started making me realise that I exist—that I exist for myself and him, and it's enough.

Nodding lightly, I took his hand as we entered the salon and one of the professional stylists came up to me, asking what he could assist us with.

"I'd like to have a haircut and get my nails done," I said, and he guided me to the client lounge, pulling out some catalogues from the receptionist's desk.

"Here are the colours and styles, you could go for if you've nothing in mind," he informed and I flipped through the pages. Everything seemed like a dream.

I always wanted to do it before joining college but bloody ghosts robbed me of my chance.

"What do you think, Treyton? I thought of getting highlights, but now I am not so sure." I poured, looking at different colours and hairstyles.

"Chipmunk," he stole my attention, and I completely let him. I am a whore for his addictive eyes. "What do you want?" What a fucking sincere guy. I know he could've told me to mind my own business, but with the kind of input he gives, will I ever find anyone so attentive to me as he is?

"I don't know, it's confusing." I agreed with my internal debate. Highlights sound great, but I wasn't so ready for the bold move. It scared me. Change scared me.

"What about getting a haircut first, and in the end, if you feel like you can add highlights, then we'll do it." He assured me. I couldn't say I wasn't nervous, but still, his presence made more sense somehow.

"You got a nice boyfriend. Pretty sure he was hard to come by. You did a great job snagging him with a lovely face such as yours."

The comment cracked a bone in my neck when I turned to see the man who witnessed my exchange with Treyton. What felt weird was his gaze on me. It made me uncomfortable, and the way he looked at Treyton made it feel as if he was a god who walked in with his servant. And, treating a servant like me who existed with a pretty face was a crime.

I am not that pretty. Just because my mom was hot as fuck woman, so I sucked her off her remaining good genes dry.

"Just because I'm kind to my girl doesn't mean I'd be fine bro-fiving some stranger who thinks passing comments about my girl earns him the right to act familiar, like sharing the same air gives him permission to parade his peasant-level manners. Stick to offering your services, not your nose in our business." Treyton was permanently pissed. And the way he talked to the man, in a complete business tone with such charm, if I was the one being insulted, maybe I wouldn't have mind it, but that's a totally me thing who is a sucker for good looks downright crazy. His face is a walking blank cheque. The sweetest and the most dangerous.

"I don't know if I appreciate a possessive man talking to me like that who decorates the word psychotic and red flag?" Was this man not in his mind? Treyton was being nice to him for the most part, I know of him. He never speaks nicely to anyone. That was out of line.

"My girl can handle the madness of her man. You should think about the face you carry because no one wants to settle for an entitled pet piglets, something even surgery cannot help. Oink. Oink." He grinned, and the man was embarrassed.

I couldn't buy a laugh at Treyton's oink expression. Oh, lord, he gets creative with his remarks everytime.

Standing, the man excused himself, and soon, another man took his place. He assisted me, taking me to the hairdresser first while Treyton sat on the seat next to mine and requested one of the guys to trim his hair from the sides.

I couldn't stop laughing when Treyton started arguing with a guy who called his hair wavy—Treyton swore it was curly.

We both had our hair done and, in the end, I was obsessed with how I looked with the butterfly cut. It looked good on my long hair that wer few inches short now.

"I'd like to get a temporary golden highlight. That spray one would do, supposedly." I admitted, appreciating myself in the mirror.

My hairdresser brought the spray highlight and perfectly

designed my copper blonde, merging with the golden.

"Chipmunk got stripes," Treyton commented, and I glared at him as we walked to the nail grooming section.

"What colour do you want?" The lady was seated behind the table and Treyton and I sat across from her in the comfy chairs.

My eyes wandered to the man for suggestions, and he threw his hands up in the air and backed out, surrendering.

"Do not ask me that, I already suggested what I can. This... Wait," Guess, he was at his limit, but he pulled his phone out and called someone.

"Hello, Mom. What kind of nail paint would suit a beginner?" He said, and I paled. Don't fucking tell me, this idiot called his mother.

The ladies around gushed about how Treyton treated me. And while, they were right there, they don't know him well enough. When he goes into anarchy mode, he gets unpredictable, and turns into a bad boy from the wrong side of the town. I had to change my locker because of this stupid man.

"It's for a girl and no, you don't need to shout and ask me questions. Now, will you help... fine, yes... The dress..." He looked at me, and I was blank. How will I come up with a mature expression when the guy beside me is actually calling his mother to get help?

For. Me.

"Red. And, white accessories most probably," he added, and then with a smile, thanked her and ended the call.

"A red and black ombre and a glossy finish. Acrylic nails. Design small white bows and add little jewels in them." He instructed the lady, whose lips curved differently as she started working on my nails.

I sat gaping at him.

It felt like he was a caring boyfriend. As if feeling that was natural with him. I couldn't handle the tickles inside my belly.

When the nails were done, I was in awe. It looked so pretty. Treyton paid, as he promised, and before I could ask for a bill, the guy decided not to have one. Reason, let's save paper. I know why he wanted to do it.

I looked hurriedly at the sum he was paying on the client monitor and noted the price on my phone. I'll pay him soon. My next recital is in two weeks, and then I'll request my professor to deduct the said amount from my paycheck and transfer it to Treyton.

"Let's go, Chipmunk." He took my hands in his, interlacing our fingers, and escorted me to the next floor, where we entered some expensive brands before going into the last boutique.

"How may I help you?" Asked one of the staff, and Treyton told her we'd like to see red dresses.

"Oh, and I'd like to look at lingerie too," I added and the lady blushed because Treyton was there, when I said it. Although, I don't understand what was embarrassing about it because it's not new. I have come with my brother in the past to buy, and Treyton has a living mother for the sake of God. More or less, he must've fucked his way through the female population enough to know what goes under the clothes like we know what goes in their pants.

Ignoring her, we walked to the inside of the store, where she brought a selection of red dresses and lingerie sets.

"Thanks. I'd try them on."

The first one had a ruffle skirt and spaghetti straps. A sweetheart neckline and thigh-high slit. It was sexy.

Gathering the courage, I walked out of the trial room and spotted Treyton sitting on the sofa, waiting for me.

His whiskeys ran over my body, admiring what he looked at, and I shivered under his addictive gaze.

"We are buying this." He grumbled, sucking in a deep breath, and I had my eyes wide as a saucepan.

"Wait. What?! That's too fast." I argued.

"I don't care, buy whatever after, we are buying this one." He deadpanned.

"Are you crazy, Treyton?" I gritted my teeth, glaring.

"Don't argue with me..." He stood up, closed the distance between us, standing foot-to-foot, and curled his index under my chin, locking his grip with the thumb, lifting my face, and leaning close to me. "One more word, Chipmunk, and I'll put you on my shoulder with this dress on, pay for it and leave."

His voice!

"But I don't have anything on under it." My stupid, very stupid self had to say it.

He sucked a deep breath, his eyes dilated, and a dark aura surrounded him.

"Fucking better." His whisper, the intensity in his eyes, and the way his taut, rigid body pressed against mine, all of it implored me to let him do exactly what he intended.

"I-I will b-buy it." Woah, I stuttered. Again.

His ego boost reached the sky, evidently.

"Good girl. Now go and show me what else is there, and if I like it on you, we are buying it. You get it?"

There was nothing to argue about. He left no room. I nodded and rushed, walking inside the trial room and shutting the doors close. My face was red in the mirror, and my hand was on my heart, calming the shit out of me. It didn't work.

Oh god, what the hell is happening with me?

I changed into a short cocktail dress. It had a floral stitched blouse, backless, and a halter neck. I loved how it accentuated my curves and even the breasts that appeared big in contrast to my slim frame which bothered me felt nice to look at.

The staff suggested a gorgeous pair of black heels, and putting it on, I walked out with a bright smile on my face, and Treyton returned my smile with his seductive one.

"Fucking gorgeous," he whispered in my ears when I came to stand in front of him.

Taken aback, I blushed, fluttering my eyes low. I like compliments.

"Chipmunk, get inside, choose lingerie quickly, and come out so we can leave these watchful eyes because I am getting impatient." His words brought confusion to me.

I couldn't comprehend, yet I hurriedly selected two sets off the rack and handed them to the lady who went to pack for me.

"I'll be wearing this one," I informed her, and she handed me an empty bag to keep my clothes in.

Treyton took my bags from me despite my revolt that he was being too nice and pulled me to Zaffiro Chiaro Di Luna, a jewellery shop, to buy stuff to go with my dress. I was looking at him as if he had grown another head at that point.

So far, as if buying me designer dresses wasn't enough, he brought me here to spend more. Was it all really a few pounds for him because then there is some problem and I have to talk to him about his overspending.

It's good that I am noting down how much he's spending on me so I can return. Luxury doesn't come free.

"Show us Ruby necklaces, earrings, and bracelets." Treyton has officially lost his cells somewhere in the mall.

"I have a new piece with me that came in today. It is a complete set of Rubies, gold, and diamonds. It has an anklet, bracelets, ring, earrings, and necklace in one complete set. Would you like to see it?"

"No."

"Yes."

Treyton and I looked at each other. He has gone crazy.

"That's too expensive, and I didn't ask you to overspend on me." I chided, trying to talk some sense into his dumb brain.

"And I said I'd pay, Chipmunk." He glared but was disrupted by the sales guy.

"What a wonderful nickname. We are offering free engraving on the set I just told you about. You can see it before making any decision. There's no harm, ma'am."

No harm. My arse. I already can see Treyton's whiskeys flaring with the engraving term. Add-on, he isn't even my boyfriend or family.

When the sales guy placed the set on the table, I think, I was sold too. It was in a feather shape. The gold plate shined eccentrically with Rubies and Diamonds.

"How much is it?" I asked, tracing the feather.

"It has beautiful, refined red that's hard to come by. This set costs 1500 gbp per ct. Adding the making charges and first-time buy discount, this would cost you 19,280 gbp."

I was looking at the man dumbfounded. What did he just say? How many pounds?

"We're buying. Engrave it with Chipmunk." Treyton was so fucking quick to make this decision.

"No. Treyton, are you crazy? I'll never be able to pay that sum back anytime soon. You know my circumstances, and that kind of money is untouchable to me, let alone a few fucking pounds. I don't want it. Please." I was on the verge of crying.

It's not that I disliked the jewellery. I fucking loved it. But paying him back, that's the issue. I cannot pay him that much without my father or brother noticing.

"I never asked for the money, Chipmunk. Like it or not, I am buying it for you. So, you can decide to throw it or donate it." His heated tone shut me up. It's crazy to think he has that kind of money on him.

He typed something on his phone and clicked his tongue before giving his credit card to the store manager. After payment, we waited in the lounge and once the engraved set came, instead of taking the bag, he pulled the case out and went on his knees, while I kept sitting and observed him as he locked the anklet around my ankles.

His fingertips glided from my leg up to my knee, where I rested my hands. Holding my wrist and bringing my knuckles close to his lips, he kissed them. I released a vulnerable breath, shaking under his touch.

He locked the bracelet and slipped the ring on my right-hand ring finger. I couldn't speak. His actions paralyzed me.

Taking the earring, he came further close to me and worked on adorning me.

I kept my gaze on him. Him licking his lips, fluttering his eyes, and clenching his jaw, wasn't supposed to tighten a knot in my belly or cause me to squish my thighs together. It just so was not supposed to happen but it was happening and I couldn't understand why.

Holding my breath, I met his eyes when his fingers circled my neck, and he clipped the pendant.

"Beautiful," he said and I was feeling it.

I felt different. I felt special for the first time in these two years of abandonment. And this feeling was comprised of a different meaning.

We were walking out of the mall, but I had no appetite anymore. Or it was more like I wanted my list to still be there so he could be there, too.

"Treyton, can you take us to some quiet place? I don't want to eat anything."

He complied, putting the helmet with care so my hair won't go disarray, and held onto my bags, hanging in front before sitting in his position and pulling me close as he started the bike and increased the speed.

We zoomed through the traffic until he brought me to a park. It was late, and hardly anyone was there.

I jumped off, kept the helmet on the bike, and walked ahead of him. He followed as we both stood by the fence separating the pond from the plane.

"Thanks a lot for today." My eyes trained on the lake, fluttering with the moon falling on the cold droplets and covering in a sheen.

"You never have to say 'thanks' to me, Chipmunk. I wasn't supposed to be okay with you, but now I am. Catering to people isn't even my thing, and you keep becoming an exception. I wasn't supposed to be scared, but this is scaring me, and I don't even know why." He looked at me while I did the same.

The moment elapsed. The crickets in the background, the gushes of wind over the water, and the thunderous palpitations in my heart synchronised.

I moved forward.

He moved by an inch.

I did until I was whisper close to him and he sealed our lips. His hands cupped my face, and I held onto the fence tightly, eyes fluttering close.

His lips were sucking on mine, tongue tracing them.

"Open your mouth, Chipmunk," he growled, and I slacked my jaw, letting him invade.

His tongue circled my mouth, lips sucking my tongue, and his hands pressing on my cheeks, pulling me close until I was wrapped around him, stealing his mouth for a breath.

His arms tightened around my waist. My fingers clawed on his shirt.

He devoured me.

I learned sweet, blissful music from his grunts and my escaping moans.

It was magical.

CHAPTER SIX

If it's okay to think how wonderful a night can be where the burn would feel better, none prepared me for the aftertaste of the poison.

The girl I kissed like she was my fucking lover wasn't supposed to betray me. She wasn't supposed to stab my father. I wasn't supposed to be waiting outside a fucking operation theatre and comforting my crying mother whilst not able to understand what fucking went wrong.

It wasn't supposed to be any of those things.

A bitter truth it was. On my face.

I still remember touching her like I owned her. Feeling her breath like she was mine to keep. Looking into her eyes like my world was there in them.

The problem? It's past tense. She isn't with me but behind the closed gates of a prison.

"How much longer would they take? David always came out of these within an hour," Mom yelled, getting impatient.

"Don't worry, Dad would be out in no time. And, Maynard is

working on the case. He won't let her or anyone involved go easy. Believe me." I kept repeating, keeping a constant lookout through Maynard, my cousin, on the phone texting me regarding any developments on the case. While I kept him updated with Dad's operation.

Grandpa, on the other hand, wasn't taking this too easy either, and my uncle, the prime minister, was moving his subordinates on the case.

Hurting a Spade would infect her so viciously that she'd never understand where the blow hit her.

Lyric Kensely. Fuck you!

Red haze. The deep shade of it clouded my vision. In the mere hours of waiting for answers, the heat of the time smouldering through the closed doors assembled fragments of many devastating revenge fuelled with hate—pure and demonic.

"Doctor..." Mom whispered, her face tracing the unparalleled pain down her cheeks. The person in scrubs and a head mask approached with a poker face.

"Mrs. Spade," he addressed as we stood up to speak to him. Mom, in a composed manner, exposed a rational domineer to attend to each of his words with care.

"The operation was successful and we must wait for forty-eight hours, keeping him under observation. The stab was deep but missed the critical area, and we will wait until his drugs wear off for any further update. You can leave him under our care, and returning in the morning is better. If any changes may happen during the night in unforeseeable circumstances, we'll inform you of it immediately." He elaborated on what to expect.

Mom sighed deeply, maintaining her composed self as the doctor left us, and she dropped in her seat, covering her face with her hands. Her shoulders trembling, her voice low, and the pain flared, escaping between her fingers as tears. She swallowed the heartbreaking medicine of accepting that Dad was hurt, unlike his previous ventures.

The continuous ring on my phone was bearing a problem though. Unfortunately, it awaited a piece of news.

"Who is it?" Mom sniffed.

"Maynard." I picked up his call, dreading what he wanted to say. For some reason, that dread was filled with a scorching agony scrapping the walls of my insides, bearing a crack for my monster to creep out in the dark, now that it had more reasons to.

"Bad news." Not a nice way to begin with. Anger seeped into his voice.

"Listening," I clenched my jaw, fisting my hand and breathing through my nostrils to find the damn composure my mother could eloquently fit in the shift of presence, but I couldn't find so easily.

"Grayson Kensley bailed her. Specifying she is a special case and medically unstable. Currently, the case is on hold, and she'll be a witness of the situation until further notice." His every word was pins and needles. I wanted to grab him by the throat and flip him to the other side of the world. He fucking said she'd not come out, but here he is, the one giving the news.

"How could you let that bitch go?!" I shouted through my phone, my eyes meeting Mom, and she gritted her teeth in disgust to hear what happened.

"I am disappointed too. They couldn't decline because her appearance didn't look good either. She wasn't in a fucking state to even tell her name when asked, how am I supposed to go against that. As far as things are considered, once uncle is up, she may be sentenced to live in an asylum," he yelled back with the same ferocity with which I questioned.

I hated hearing him. I hated each word of his.

Dad wouldn't be getting justice. That cross-wired my brain, but she will go to an asylum? It suddenly hit me. That thought left a rancid taste in my mouth. I fucking hated hearing the conclusion. And all of this back and forth didn't just tire me, it confused and fucked with my mind.

The best revenge, they say, is served cold. In my case, I'll serve piping hot and viciously brutal. I wasn't the bully, I just fucking hated her. She was my enemy, the drive that pushed me forward.

When her conscience died, so did my conviction that bloomed something unnamed. That nameless entity burned inside me with her name on the recipient list.

"You sure? This is a no-return point, and from here, it would escalate." Hunter squeezed my shoulder, waiting for a response. I was supposed to give one, but I couldn't find it in myself to regret. I wasn't regretting a single damn thing.

"You are in this or not? I don't fucking need your concern to think with the brain card when preferably you shouldn't be even using it much for the sake of others, considering how scarcely it's present for your own need." I rasped. My glare imbued with that hedonist clawing on the surface again.

Easy, boy. You'll be let out in a moment.

"Just do what you deem fine." He turned his head around, closing the door behind us. The bat thick in my hand, I dragged it across the floor to the most cherished piano of the madness. Heard it belonged to her mother, who was once a graduate of our college. Luna Kensley doesn't exist anymore. This holds a vital essence of her memories to Lyric.

Swinging the thick metal bat in the air, the finesse grapples over the keys, strumming incoherent and ugly tune like its user. This is the very piano Lyric claimed was disgraced because I fucked a girl in front of it. However, today she'd lose it for her fucked up mistake.

Another hit jamming in the metal and leaving marks of anarchy behind. The blood lust, the red haze, and the anger unparalleled surrounded me. The beast breaking free from within and merging with me as one.

People have faces. Everyone moves with a mask in the crowd. I was no different, but what stood out was all the faces within me becoming one, causing my beloved anarchy. I find no greater joy other than this, and when the thought that it might be possible something could annihilate me, her face burned in the vibrant flames.

The burn in my chest was no different from the burn that heated beneath my skin with her thoughts and licked in the temptation of authority. A special emotion that made me believe I'd end up owning her. Every bit of her.

Now, she'll tremble with the very thought of my name around her.

"It's destroyed, Treyton. Let the damn piano go." Hunter took a hungry puff from his cigarette roll and released it into the air, the heavy smoke screening him.

"I know, but it's merely enough. I want to barge into her house and choke her to death, if possible. You know what, I have a better idea than that, so very great ones that'd make her regret living." The smirk on my face clung as I tilted my head, pulled my lighter out, and stepped back from the piano.

Hunter opened a plastic bottle he carried. A kerosene bottle. Pouring every drop of the liquid on the surface, and in between the chords and strings of the piano, he stepped back, leaving the stage to me.

"Fuck you, Lyric Kensely." Tossing the lighter over the piano, I witnessed the beautiful colours radiating through the flames and wiping every inch of the thing she cherished.

Hereafter, it begins, the hell I've decorated intricately for her. Every piece there is embellished with my own hands, especially for the guest of honour. *The prodigy pianist, Lyric Kensely.*

CHAPTER SEVEN

My first kiss happened when I was 14. It went bad, not that the boy was a bad kisser but because I had an overly possessive and protective brother who wouldn't believe his baby sister wanted her first kiss. And Grayson being Grayson, thought I was forced, and with the group of his friends, beat the shit out of the boy I kissed. Since then, boys have been scared to talk to me, and my love life has become hard, placid, and meh.

That wasn't the full stop for me or Grayson, either. I went and had a make-out session with his jock friend when I was 16, who participated in my first kiss chaos, and that jock couldn't ever play in the field again.

History repeats. Before I could analyse, something big happened. The ghost murder of the fifteenth.

Just because for one person life stops doesn't mean for everyone it'll. None can blame the loved ones of the victim for simply living and existing in a different world than theirs, for having a life they failed to have. So, I never dwelled on that thought and blamed none. As time passed, it worsened because I had no one to blame for my misery.

Objectively, things were still better than the worst until Grayson couldn't contact his girlfriend, and only later, we came to know she fucked his enemy.

He loved her. I know this. I've seen my brother going head over heels for her. She was a sweet soul or not, now that I've my brother's heart on the line. After that, Grayson's chestnut browns dimmed. The person who always stood far more overbearing for his 6'4 height with exorbitant muscles and being the college boxing club's black horse never was the same.

I've seen him drunk on many nights, and ivory skin tanner than mine exhibiting bruises and cuts, bleeding on occasions when Dad wasn't supposed to be home.

My mother's death changed him much more than it did me. I was young and naive, and growing up, the realisation of not having as many memories with her as Grayson hurts, too. There is no competition. He was her beloved baby, and a huge piece was ripped from him with her loss. It landed on Dad to cut his grief short and control his son, who was drowning in misery and dealing with it by bullying.

I still remember he had a long conversation with Grayson in his home office while I was sitting outside the door waiting for them to be out. A long night; it was both heavy, depressing, and questioning in so many ways. Dad made up his mind not to grieve Mom anymore and always remember her with a smile. Grayson joined boxing to deal with his anger issues developed from the trauma of loss and stress, and I...

I chose to become the forgotten symphony and keep my mother alive, which binds us three together as one family.

"Don't blame others for what you're going through," became Grayson's monologue, and instead of helping me out like he used to, he joined the forces of the chaos that troubled me.

Despite that, when tonight he dropped the pill bottle and watched me chew and swallow the bitter medicine, I smiled. I smiled, huge and proud. It could've been flirty, considering my cheeks were warm, and his brows curved up in confusion. He was trying his best to read.

Judging by his looks, his first attention was drawn to the bags with me, an expensive dress I walked in, and from designer shoes to nails, everything seemed to wreck his nerves haywire.

"What's the occasion? Something good happened?" He rolled his eyes around the room, and I grinned. Grinned like Treyton, who was holding my hand so often, it seemed he'd take it with him. The idea sounds hilarious but given Treyton Spade, the possibility of his favourite word 'anarchy' could be endless.

I heard him once talking to Hunter about how he loves anarchy the most.

"What will you do, if I tell you?" I grabbed my pyjamas from the closet and walked into the bathroom to change. Door shut behind me, and I know, Grayson is still waiting outside. He may have changed in the last two years but he's never stopped from his nightly routine of taking charge and putting me in bed, tucking me like a baby.

I changed into my pyjama shorts and tank top and walked out, still grinning.

"Nothing. You're smiling like that after a long time, given tonight will be the beginning of the fifteenth you dread the most every month. It's good to see," his poker face highlighted the most important event that initially was the reason driving me to beg Treyton to fulfil my wishes.

I gulped, and suddenly, the happy bubble blasted inside me. My smile faded. I was so proud of smiling seconds ago.

The turnaround time of my happiness was low. I could barely feel my body; the fear crawled in my shadows. It flowed beneath my feet and consumed me. I could feel the chills of the night, be aware of the crickets in the garden, and the wind that blew outside my window terrified me. I was scared of being alone in this room.

The arms of the clock ticked.

10:55 pm.

Tick.

Tock.

10:56 pm.

Tick.

Tock.

The visible stretch of the time snagging the light I somehow begged to have deflated my heart, blooming with joy and suppressed with extreme anxiety.

"Damn it. Sorry. Are you alright? Shouldn't have brought that up." His apologies fell on deaf ears becauseI wasted no time slipping into bed and pulling the quilt over my head. Hiding from the ghost of the fifteenth manifesting tonight.

I heard Grayson closing the windows of my room, checking the lock on the balcony doors, and confirming for the second time that each lock worked and was in place. He does that all the time. Everyday.

"Goodnight, Lyric." He kissed my forehead over the quilt and walked out. Locking the door on his way out with a loud thud.

The air in my room was silent. I could hear every drop of noise that knocked on the window pane of my room. The only evident voice was of the wall clock above my bed.

I twisted. Turned. Deprived of sleep. The deplorable anxiety creeps under my bed. Creeks of loud noises from the gushing wind continuously knocking again, and again on the window creeps me out. Among them, the resonating voice of my clock, I tried to ignore was the most prominent.

Again.

Again.

Again.

Again.

I peeked out of my quilt with a shaky breath. My feet and hands were numb from the effect of the pill I take every night. If a zombie can move and is considered half alive, then my nightly pill turned me into a corpse. I could feel it taking effect on my limbs and joints. The apex of my fingers losing their sensation.

My lids were heavy. My eyes were watery, dilating from the stench of the drug infused in my blood.

Tick.

Tock.

I panted, breathing becoming a difficult chore as my movements restricted. The clock on my nightstand marked the beginning of my dreaded nightmare.

12:01 am.

Tick.

12:02 am.

Tock.

I whimpered, shaking until the pounding in my head subsided. Gradually, my body became languid.

My eyes were half open. My body rested with its own command.

I kept looking at my nightstand.

Tick.

1:10 am.

Tock.

Hallucinations overcame. The similar images of every night of the fifteenth. As it happened, always.

I closed my eyes for a moment or tried to. And I kept on closing it through the creek on the flooring, the cluttering of the windows, and the tremor that now started to grow loud in my head, originating from my ears.

Tick.

My head hurts.

The sensation of someone tracing my face was there, but I couldn't open my eyes. Not right now. It's not my time. My hallucination is yet to manifest completely.

Tock.

My throat hurts.

The touch feels cold on my body. The curve of muscles holding me in a tight grip imprinted from my hallucinations.

Tick.

My ears hurt.

There were whispers. Knocks. Murmurs. My hallucinations are taking their form slowly.

Tock.

My legs hurt.

I can feel something hard beneath me. It's happening. My hallucinations have manifested in a touchable entity.

Tick.

My arm hurts.

I am being dragged. The cold street. The smell of the air drenched in dews of spring. The setup of my hallucinations.

Tock.

My stomach hurts.

The nauseating stench of burning flesh. Another important figment of my hallucinations.

Tick.

My back hurts.

I can feel my eyes taking control. My hallucinations have completely manifested. It's taken a dreadful form.

My hallucinations are real.

Tock.

Everything hurts.

I forced my eyes open. Finding myself again on the cursed street in front of the old and abandoned shop.

A whimper escaped my lips. A tear trickled down the corner of my eyes. My body, which felt lifeless, regained its consciousness.

I want to disappear.

"Help me." The same scream but like every other time, it's different today, too.

This time, it's masculine.

Strong hands grabbed my ankle. The reality of my hallucinations simmered inside me. I pushed, forcing my leg out of the grip. My face slowly became a crying mess of tears and snot.

I kicked, stood, and tried to run away like every other time.

History repeats.

I am always making futile attempts to get nowhere.

With blurry eyes, I looked behind me at the guy dragging his body over the tarmac, leaving a blood trail. His face was caked in blood and mud, his nails chipped off, and his eyes begged me, crying as he tried to reach me.

I stood there for a grave moment before he reached, and his touch obstructed my panic. Red Hands grabbed my ankles again, but this time, I kicked in the man's face.

Maybe I can run. This time maybe, it'd be different.

Although, that very hope short lived. The ghost. The ghost of the dead appeared. His face burned, teeth protruding out of his face structure, and eyes bulged. I screamed as the ghost of the man ran towards me, and by the thread of my hair twisted in the curve of his fingers, he pushed me on the ground.

I fell, taking the hit as my elbow scraped, bleeding, and my head buzzed with the physical wound.

Reeling in pain, I watched the ghost murdering the man on the ground with multiple stabs by a crooked knife until he was dead.

My breath was short; my limbs struggling to move, and the happenings of every fifteenth of every month for two years from the first night kept repeating.

Soaking hands in the blood, the ghost of the man started writing on the wall in big letters, *Help me.*

When I thought he was finished or nearly done by his last dip in the blood, loud sirens from the cop's car surrounded the area.

I cried loud. "HELP. ME." Choking. Swallowing the tears that reached the corners of my face.

The ghost of the man was alert, peeked around and opened the shop's door, sneaking inside.

In the small span, cops infiltrated the space. Half the batch ran to the body of the dead victim and the other half towards me.

I was covered in the victim's blood, but that might not be the only aspect suspicious enough to have me cuffed.

The other aspect was the medicine I took. The painful pills. They were not normal, I knew. I still swallowed them, knowing I had no choice.

In the final phase, the black dots take the shape of a fog and play with my mind.

I closed my eyes, trying to breathe through the thick fog covering me, the threads holding me tight, crawling in my mouth, cinching around me.

I gasped, trying my best to scratch the threads binding me.

"Fuck!!" A hurtful screech burned my ears.

I pushed through the threads and felt my hand over a cold metal. Was it the knife left by the ghost?

I can use it.

I can use it to cut the threads.

Grabbing, I plunged the knife deep in the ball of threads, and a loud shout halted the commotion in the air. My blurry vision slowly cleared, and I watched with terrified eyes what manifested from my fears was not what reality was.

My hands wrapped around the knife plunged inside the chest of a police man. The blood flowing, painting my flesh red.

Red was everywhere.

"Restrain her."

Someone shouted, and two men in uniform grabbed me by

the shoulders, pushing me down on the ground and cuffing my hands on my back.

I tried to break free, not the right move, but under the fading influence of the pills, I had no fair judgement left.

This isn't what I hoped for. It isn't what I wanted!

Hauled into the police car, I was driven past the flashing cameras of the media. When we reached the station, I was locked inside the temporary prison.

In this terrific situation, I remained silent, knowing my words could act against me. Being a lawmaker's daughter, I knew how things worked. If only I knew how things shouldn't have led to this.

My eyes trained on my hands, covered in blood. Blotches of red drench my pyjamas and splashes dry on the skin of my feet, arms, and thighs.

I was scared of seeing the red and cried, hugging myself.

I don't want to be alone.

"I am scared." I whimpered through my trembling lips, trying to clear my head space.

The air was still. There was no commotion like before. I hated how pathetic I was. I hated I hurt someone innocent. I hated myself.

"Why I cannot disappear?"

I watched my shadow clinging to my side in the chilly prison cell, as it battled against the threads on the wall under the faint light.

"Don't fight it," I begged, trying to reach myself and finding no use in this. I will be convicted for attempted murder only if the person whom I don't know killed comes out alive. But if they don't, then I'll be charged with murder.

"Come out. You're going to be interrogated." The thick voice of the officer waiting by the small opening of the cell bars dictated me. I looked up, terrified, and could see his eyes red with a stroke of hate cast under his chin that tipped in revulsion as I took the support of the wall I was sitting against.

On my trembling feet, I pushed myself up, trying to walk.

I fell miserably.

And it frustrated the man. So much so, he entered inside, grabbed me by the arm, and hauled me out of the cell.

The air was still. No commotion. My mind was blank. No harmony played.

I am a musician but no music came to me. Corpse. Yes, I am a corpse. They don't need a symphony.

Entering the room and sitting on the chair with my hands cuffed in front, I faced the police officer. He was an elderly man with pepper salt hair and thick nerd glasses dominating most of his face, hiding his features.

He had a small recording device in his hand, which he started and spelled his name, designation, date, and time of the interrogation before proceeding to keep the recorder in the middle of the table.

"Your lawyer is here, waiting outside, and with the permission of the guardian, under submitted papers, we consider you're going through a medical treatment. Now, please, speak your name. Spell every syllable loud and clear."

As instructed, I nodded and, in a broken voice, pronounced my name, spelling each letter given to me and present on my legal documents after stuttering for long to remember what my name was. My mind was blank. I could hardly think through.

"My first question. What were you doing in the restricted location, prohibited to enter by the police in the middle of the night?" No emotions, no facial expressions, and it became so hard for me to make eye contact and keep myself from trembling or crying, again. I wasn't even a crier.

"I... I don't... Know. As my previous statements were given for every night of the fifteenth, this stands similar. I don't know how I was there, but I know how the murder happened. It was a ghost of the dead man who died ten years ago in the fire accident." What was it in my voice that made the officer click his tongue, annoyed and ignoring my statement in relevance to all the previous ones I have given so far, I don't know, but it must be repulsive for him to hear it.

"Can you tell me where the ghost went? As reported by the patrolling officers, the cameras in the vicinity and on the location stopped working an hour before the occurrence of the murder. If you witnessed the ghost, then you know where it went." There was anger bubbling down his throat and vibrant in his eyes.

"Yes. It went inside the abandoned shop."

"Do. Not. Lie. We have checked inside the shop. There is no escape route or blind spot. Nothing was found inside," he claimed, and I shook my head.

"No, it can't be possible. I saw with my own eyes he went there inside the shop." My altercation had no impact on him. He was assured, I was lying.

"Ok. Let's move forward. We, for instance, believe what you're saying is true, but can you explain your actions? Why did you stab Deputy Commissioner David Spade in the chest?"

I paled. My hands and feet froze hearing him. Did he say David Spade, Treyton's father?

Horror filled my eyes. How could that be possible? How could I do that?

"I am sorry," I cried, tears streaming down my cheeks. "I didn't want to. I was trying to protect myself."

"You agree, Lyric Kensely, you tried to murder David Spade when he was there to help you?!" He slammed his hand aggressively on the table, losing his composure and hiccupping, I said what I shouldn't have.

"Yes."

I am scared.

Help me.

The altercation went on for long when another officer took over the interrogation.

When it ended, I was bailed out with strict instructions to remain in the city, and never leave until I'm told. I should be present for any surprise or appointed investigation for the case.

I finally walked out to meet my brother, who was standing with an unreadable face.

I am scared.

"Let's go," he groused, holding my hand as we exited but stopped short when I saw the lady from today, who stood by Treyton's side marching towards us.

She saw me, stepped forward, and before my brother or I could contemplate, she slapped me across my face.

"David wanted to protect you. How could you do that? Why you stabbed my husband when he had nothing to do with you or your fucking madness?" She shouted, and I understood why it happened. She is Treyton's mother.

When she voiced, every officer's head bowed. They claimed no argument for her action, and I didn't blame her either. Not her or the officers who turned a blind eye.

"We'll meet soon, Mrs. Spade." Grayson addressed her professionally and pulled me out of there.

We were sitting in the car, ignoring the reporters storming at us while the bodyguards kept them at bay. In the group of thousands, I spotted him through the car window.

Treyton was in the corner, his thumb flicking the lighter spark wheel, and he looked murderous. His eyes followed mine. They met. Addicting eyes were catching brutal flames. There was hate, enmity, and extreme revulsion.

I never wanted this. I never wanted the man I kissed to hate me.

I wanted something magical. Not this. Not to become his father's murderer. I don't want this.

"I am sorry." I cried.

"You've got a lot coming forward, Lyric, and this doesn't even begin with the fire you caused us to tend to." Grayson's heated words and Treyton fading in the crowd, I hated it all.

I am scared.

Help me.

CHAPTER EIGHT

"Cookie?" I offered like any other day, sending my gratitude with the sweet nothingness. He could've accepted them too, if not for the news reporters painting my crime on every screen.

The driver, whose name I don't know yet, his elderly smile and good morning face captured in my memory, declined the same cookie he always accepted. It saddened me how just a week might've passed since the gruesome incident, but things went from bad to worse.

"I understand. Thanks for the ride." I left.

Stepping into the hallway came as a breath of fresh air from the isolation of the room I'd been living in since the past week. While it was nearly impossible to convince my father and brother to let me go and attend my classes, given the multiple confrontations and interrogations I went through each passing day, taking a toll on me, I still was able to make it happen.

However, there was a catch to it. I must call my father at every two-hour gap and meet Grayson on campus whenever he demands without any excuse.

Surveillance.

I don't find it bothersome. Dad and Grayson haven't confronted me about what happened in a different aspect, and I just told them what occurred, as always. If they believe, they'll try to find out what happened to me and why I was on that street, but if they don't, I'm scared to imagine the consequences.

"We've to study with a killer?" Someone whispered as I crossed them, my head down in shame. I wanted to ignore everything, from walking in the whispering halls to the classroom, where the chatter wouldn't stop.

Holding my breath, I sat at the back of the classroom, occupying my permanent table, only to find my portion spray-painted in red. There was a monster drawn and a knife in its hand. *Psycho, killer, and die bitch* written in bold letters.

Taking in a deep breath, I snorted loudly in the air and looked at the people who gave me bombastic side eyes.

"At least you all could've asked for a favour from the fine arts department. A play school kid draws better than you all."

They couldn't say anything or weren't given the opportunity because Professor Danbury entered the class. Silence followed by good morning, and he instantly started the vocal training lessons, not entertaining any murmurs that were spoken about me.

I never cared. Why would I?

Tormentors are weak in their minds. They like bullying people because they don't have the guts to face someone head-on.

The classes rolled in, yet I remained anchored in my spot until I was set free. Just as I was leaving the room, Grayson made his way over to me.

"Where you'll head to?" As nonchalant as ever.

Despite the blooming rumour in the college, the golden boy was still a golden boy. No one cared he was my brother. Their admiration ran deeper than their disgust for the misfit, crazy daughter of the mayor.

"Music room." My eyes cast low in submission and guilt. I couldn't see his expression and dreaded what kind of face he'd be making. I hate seeing him hate me.

"I'll escort you," he offered, and I accepted, and followed, just a step behind his every move.

"Fucking pests." Grayson grumbled under his breath.

I don't know whether it was meant for the growing murmurs as we passed by the people filling the halls or for the people whose eyes looked monstrous, hawking me. I could feel the heat of their stares burning my back.

"We're here. I'll come pick you up later." He left me outside the music room.

I was nervous before entering, but the vacant room eased me. Keeping my bag, my eyes took in the new furniture and corners of the space. It might be the same colour, design, and style, but I know it's new. When the cellist accidentally bumped her cello against the mirror, I remember there being a small crack. This one doesn't have it. And the curtains had some threads coming out, but now they don't. It's crazy how I am gifted with this nuisance of intelligence. This very photographic memory has cost me everything.

My gift is my curse.

Struggling to catch my breath, I approached the piano. I moved closer, but then I just stood there, unable to take another step.

What the heck? What's all this? This isn't right... No... No... No... No!!

I whirled around and sprinted to the door, anxiety flooding me from the terrifying image I had just witnessed. How could there be a new piano? Where was my mother's piano?

Rattling with the doorknob, I pulled it open to call for the janitor or any staff who uses the room other than me or might know where my piano went.

This room wasn't special to me. It was the knowledge of playing my mother's piano that made this room exist with a meaning, a solace for me in this college. It was the only reason I wanted to come and attend my classes so I could play it.

I dashed through the crowd, feeling their eyes consume me, tearing me apart with their stares. My cheeks were damp, a strange moisture I couldn't explain, and my vision blurred, as if the world was slipping away from me.

"Miss, do you know where my Piano is?" I questioned the woman who always comes by the music room to clean after I leave from my practice session.

"Uh... You... Um... I... I don't know." She hesitated and then turned away her gaze, focusing in another direction, and explicitly declining to know about my mother's piano.

"No. You must know where it went. Where? Tell me." I argued.

She walked away, shouting at me. "I don't know where that garbage went, and I don't want to know. You have a new piano, so why make a fuss about that piece of trash? Go and do your work. Don't cause a nuisance, you crazy bitch."

"That's not a piece of trash! It's my mother's piano!" I yelled at her, realising my voice choked. Sniffing, I ran back to the room and crumbled to the ground. My knees gave up when I saw Treyton there, grinning like a maniac as the new piano burned to ashes. He flicked the lighter in his hand, tilting his neck and looking at me in amusement.

I cried. My piano or not, music was still special to me, and he was burning the only source of self-assurance I had. He was burning the piano.

"No!" I shouted and sprinted towards the piano on fire. The brilliance of the flaming heat was sensational on my skin. Standing right there, I couldn't touch it because Treyton, at the very moment, wrapped me in his strong arms from behind, restricting my movements and forcing me to watch the instrument burn.

I cried, thrashed against him, and begged, but he wouldn't let me go.

"Please. I beg you, please don't burn it. Don't do it."

"Chipmunk, there are so many things you've to beg for. To apologize for, and this fucking burnt piano doesn't even begin with it." His voice resonated vividly in my ears.

"I am sorry," I tried apologising, knowing why he loathed me.

"Chipmunk, that was quick, but no. I don't fucking need your apology." Anguish. Scars. He was enjoying every bit of it.

"What can I do for you? What will make you change your opinion of me?"

He let me go, and I slumped on the floor in a heap of messy emotions. He took no time before tossing some papers and a pen on my lap.

I picked them in my trembling hands and looked at him, and

back at the paper, reading the entire document to only conclude it was the replica of the same paper I sent him as a joke with minor changes having a major impact. They nearly meant slavery at this point. He changed me from the provider party to the receiver and put himself as the master. What I meant as a joke back then was biting me in my arse.

"What do you mean by this? I don't get it." My eyes gradually stopped tearing, and hollowness reclaimed. Replacing the light I hardly captured and trapped in there.

"What do you think? It has the same purpose as you meant, with slight changes. While yours meant to humiliate me, this from me means to destroy you. Now fucking sign, Lyric Kensely, if you have even a tad bit of awareness for your fucking actions. How you plunged a knife through my father's chest when all he meant was to protect the victim and witnesses." He growled, holding my jaw as he leaned close to my face.

Once, this beautiful face leaned to snatch my breath away for many reasons. Those addictive whiskeys drunk me into a magical trance. Replacing that playful enmity, he gave me this: a monster.

"I will not." Gritting, I trashed the papers in the fire.

He didn't stop. He smirked, looked at the paper burning with the piano, and tsked, licking his lips.

"You shouldn't have done that. You escaped an easy punishment, Chipmunk. I considered a lot in case my father might've not opened his eyes. I thought going easy, but you like it rough."

His eyes met mine. The whiskeys burned in the bright reflection of fire as he stood up, walked past me, and left. The hedonist I just saw in those orbs was elated, even happy that I did that. I chose to refuse because breaking the broken would be no fun.

My nervous nerves kicked in; I ran to my backpack, pulled the medicine bottle out, and popped the tablets, crushing between my teeth as my brother stormed in, his eyes pitch black from anger.

"Why The Fuck Did You Burn The Piano?!"

"I didn't."

I repeated endlessly to my shadow that sunk deep into the dark under my bed.

Telling the truth had no use. Grayson didn't believe me, not when Treyton and other students walked in, using the fire extinguisher to put out the fire and Treyton confessing, he saw me hiding a lighter in my bag. I had none. I never carried one, too. Although, no use because Treyton already had a lighter sneaked in my bag, when I was gone inquiring about my mother's piano.

News flashed soon. Dad was angry, Grayson lost his shit and dragged me back home, and the vice chancellor called Dad, suggesting for me to be locked at home.

I have paid the consequences. I wasn't leaving home anymore or wouldn't be going to until it was settled on what should be done with me.

Hugging myself, scared, I wondered about everything. The most itching thought was Treyton's behaviour towards me, and to back that ill-intent was my doing that started the dirty game of red hands between us.

Red Hands. I remember playing it as a little girl. A game that tests reflexes and speed, but also the other person's determination to hurt, and your own endurance. If you're not paying attention, before you know it, it's game over. But I don't remember when my life started playing it with me.

My body slipped into numbness as I lay there hearing the voice from the wall clock.

Tick.

The endless voice or not, it doesn't matter anymore. In the curtains of night, a shadow unlike my own that runs and hides appeared over the gates of my balcony. The door was closed. No intruder could come inside. Not even the manifestation of my hallucinations that slips in, kidnaps me and scratches another tally on the wall of my abused body.

Tock.

I breathe, taking harsh deep breaths as the door opens and the silhouette of a sublime young man walks in.

Tick.

"Who?" I screeched in a low voice, trying not to make this an issue of the house. I shouldn't trouble anyone. I don't want my father to deal with more of the hassle. To put my brother to shame.

Tock.

It didn't speak. The dark silhouette in the pitch-black room crawled on the bed, hovering over my body and sitting on my stomach, trapping me between its sturdy legs.

Chills sizzled the surface of my skin. I tried breathing. Exercising power to keep myself conscious of my situation. Forcing to stay in the moment. Fighting the strong drug in my system.

"Who are you?" I tried again.

Tick.

The silhouette leaned down, soft lips grazing my jaw, inclining towards the arc of my ear.

A shaking breath left my lips when its tongue licked my ear, and teeth nibbled my lobe.

"Who are you?" This time, my voice was desperate, rattled, and terrified.

Tock.

Don't show your enemy your weakness they say, but lying unmoving was my biggest weakness. I am harmless.

It moved away, hands grabbed my jaw in a tight grip, and abruptly, my vision cleared. Despite the darkness, I knew who it was.

"Treyton."

He didn't speak, tightened his grip, and my lips puckered, mouth forced open. He pushed two fingers inside my mouth, rubbing my saliva over my tongue.

His fingers slipped further inside, and my eyes watered, a gagging reflex hitting the back of my throat. He tipped my head back and pushed in his fingers, touching the back of my throat.

"Breathe from your nose," he growled. His voice was low and authoritative.

I tried doing that, ignoring the burn in my lids as tears slipped past my eyes and focused on breathing through my nose.

He kept rubbing over my tongue and pushing his fingers in and out of my mouth in a slow, torturous rhythm.

"Ready for punishment, Chipmunk?" There was greedy excitement behind his aggressive tone. The voice that sounded music to my ears suddenly scared me of the unknown.

He pulled his fingers out, leaving my mouth a mess of dripping saliva from the corner of my lips.

He moved closer, up over my body, until I felt him moving before something soft and hard touched my lips.

Cognizance of what it was inserted a shot of adrenaline in my system, and I wiggled under him. He grabbed my jaw again with one hand and choked me with another.

Gasping for air, I opened my mouth wide, and he pushed his cock inside, filling my mouth. His hand released my throat and pressed over the wall, above me behind my bed, as he slacked his hip, moving inch after inch, deep inside my throat.

"Chipmunk, if you don't want your brother and father seeing you choking on my cock to death, don't try anything that'll piss me off. Follow as I say, and you might love your punishment just as much," he groused, and the thought of humiliating my family annihilated me.

I loosened my limbs and let him take control as he pulled and pushed, the tip hitting my throat. Breathing through my nostrils, my ears picked up his grunts as he moved, using my mouth to give himself a blow job.

"Use that tongue. Lick." He instructed, and I did. It was humiliating and nothing like when he kissed me.

Unlike the butterflies that tickled my stomach, nausea bubbled in my throat. I licked the underside of his dick and gently grazed my teeth over his foreskin. The humming of satisfaction from him did nothing to me. There was no sensation in my body other than revulsion as the drug practically paralyzed me.

He increased his speed, and my tongue tried matching the rhythm. He came inside my mouth.

I coughed, spilling his cum all over me, half swallowing and half on my face, chest, and my pillow.

"Fuck, dirty little thing. You made a mess. Beg for forgiveness with gratitude, or I'll have to call your father to clean it up. Should I?" The threat was so convincing that I shook my head and addressed him in a hoarse voice.

"I am sorry. Please forgive me." I waited for him to respond and be done with me.

However, in the dwelling darkness in which my shadow resides, a spark of flying flame dusted and illuminated.

I saw him. His beautiful face and hauntingly addictive eyes glowing. He was sitting on my legs, and the lighter burned at a safe height above my exposed stomach. My pyjama was in disarray for his feast.

He stared into my eyes. The horror was superior to the ghost of the fifteenth.

A wax stick angled over the flaming lighter dripped on my stomach. I winced, moaning in pain.

"Say, please, sir. I'm sorry, sir. And thank you for your punishment." His dictatorial behaviour forced me into submission.

It hurts. I still coerced myself to say those words. Remembering the terms and rules of the BDSM document I sent him, aware that he wanted me to act accordingly.

"Sorry, sir... I apologise for making a mess... Thanks for the punishment." I said, stealing deep breaths in between.

I moaned as he spilled the hot wax on my stomach, the burning sensation hurting but not severe or scalding.

"Good girl." He hummed in delight and stopped pouring hot wax. The light doused, and darkness embraced us, again.

"Thank you, sir," I panted, clenching my jaw.

"Savour your reward, Chipmunk."

I felt him. His warm tongue licking and sucking the burn on my stomach. It must be edible wax he used, but I hardly know a thing or two about anything of this world of sin he hauled me into for pure infliction of power and redemption.

His tongue dipped in my naval and out, biting and kissing the burns. His hand pushed my thighs apart. He shifted and leaned down, throwing my legs over his shoulder.

"Ahh... Treyton..." This voice was different than the voices that left me. It came out sensual and erotic when he started sucking on my clit over my pyjamas. I couldn't move my hands, and there was a desperate itch in my limbs to hold him.

"Ahh..."

He bit me over the fabric, and my entire body jolted. I've never felt anything like this, both revolting and disgusting, but a small, entirely unknown part of me divulged in the pleasure his mouth scored on my skin.

"Thank you, sir. Anything else, and you'll be punished, Chipmunk. Am I audible?" He growled, pressing his demand in his words.

"Y-Yes. Y-Yes, Sir." I moaned, feeling his mouth back on me. My shorts were drenched with his saliva and my liquid heat.

"Ohhhh... Fuck..."

He bit again when I cursed, and a strained knot inside my stomach slackened. My thighs trembled, and I came. He pressed his tongue, smothering my cum into my shorts.

As if lifted out of my body, I felt everything loose. He wasn't there, but his message poisoned my hearing.

"You cry for me. You laugh for me. You die for me. And you will live for me. I am your master, your owner from this moment, Lyric Kensely. Am I clear?"

"Y-Yes, Sir."

Fuck you, Treyton Spade. I fucking hate you.

CHAPTER NINE

She is hiding. Again.

I shouldn't have touched an innocent sin. No. I should've devoured it. Left on my mercy, I should've had my meal until satisfied. But I didn't. I couldn't when wrath slowly diminished, and I could hear her sweet, sinister moan corrupting me. It was her voice, but my chest felt wide, full, and complete, beating in a synchronised rhythm with hers. And that sets an alarm. It shouldn't have happened. Not with the girl I punished like I loved her and rewarded like I hated her.

"Found your Chipmunk." That insufferable bastard.

Rolling my eyes, I ignored him.

Hunter is a big guy, sporting the exact number of muscles to be a part of the boxing team instead of football. He squeezed in between the ruckus called basketball team I had on my booty call list, who came to divert my attention and were supposed to be hilarious. Although, my booty call failed to do one thing they were meant to.

I couldn't pretend to care about sitting space and

arrangements. My mind was a scattered mess, like a thousand difficult pieces of a puzzle that seemed easy to put together, but once I started, it became ugly.

Hunter smirked, catching my attention.

"Where?!" My voice, fucking desperate and void of any emotion, silenced the others crowding the cafeteria table.

"She's back in college. Where I saw her... Hmmm... A difficult task to remember?" My brawny whore needs something for him to be begging attention like this.

"Don't play with me, Hunter, and if it's difficult, then what's easy, reading your obituary?" I warned him, fisting my hands to control the urge to punch a hole in his face.

"Someone is getting cocky," the guy sitting opposite Hunter, laughed.

Hunter doesn't like sass from strangers, and I'll not be attending this unknown person's funeral. I don't even know him, for the sake of God. He isn't on the team either.

"Better shut up before he castrates you," I warned, assessing Hunter, who stared at the guys with a hooded gaze and fuckers with no backbone cowered in fear.

"I thought you would be done with the girl?" Garry, one of the guys on my team, spoke. He looks ignorant to his chick from the tennis club, sucking his neck.

I don't mind that, but I mind them dry-humping in front of me. Yes, their slurping sound, I mind that cringe. Very. Literally and figuratively.

"Why should I?" My glare focused on him as he gulped, looking away instantly.

"Didn't she kill your father?" Another piece of artwork.

"Attempted. She did that under the influence of medicine. My father's awake and has given his statement that she didn't intend to harm, and it was an accident." I don't know why I am like that. They're bad-mouthing Lyric, but it offended me. Just to be fair to my conscience, I don't fucking admire someone speaking ill of my woman.

I claimed her mine the previous night, a week ago, so I'll only get to be her judge, jury, and executioner. And everybody else gets to watch only at the expense of my permission. Which none will ever have, not until they are reborn as Lyric herself.

"You're weird," says Garry's girlfriend.

"Coming from someone like you amazes me." I hate her. She fucking instigated some of many rumours about Lyric just because this chick never caught the attention of some senior Lyric was close to. They fucking loved music, that's their common ground, nothing else. How could she be jealous of that?!

I'm not. Maybe.

But, Chipmunk is talented, so she gets the attention, willing or not. If this chick had a problem, she should've worked it to make herself the limelight or known in which basket to score. Bad reputation and sabotaging aren't part of the way of work to have someone's attention.

"That girl is nothing but an eyesore and an easy opening for bullying." She snarled, and I was irritated before half the conversation was over.

I try not to touch girls with ill intention, but this bitch is making her name move up my list to burn idiots and free this world from pests' anarchy.

"Or maybe not. She just dropped a can of paint on the girl who pushed her down the stairs. I don't call that being bullied." Hunter whistled, smirking wide and enjoying the astounding expressions of the dumb-fucks.

Not everyone on the team was, but some could be a handful, and Garry and his Chick tops the chart.

"Pushed? Was she hurt?" I focused on Hunter, ignoring the waste of air.

"Not telling. You can check on her." He cocked his brow, reading my lips that never moved, but he understood the tsunami I was engulfed in.

"You better pray, Hunter; Scarlett won't receive a letter back home addressing her boyfriend's funeral. Cause of death, burned from fucking a lamp post on fire."

I walked away, my aim to find Lyric at any cost.

Those fuckers don't get to bully her. Only I will be her tormentor and saviour. She has me as a choice or none.

Hurled out of my thoughts, my phone vibrated with a message notification.

Brawny Whore: *In the library. Hiding.*

Fucker could've easily told me back there but chose to hold his nose high up his arse.

I entered the library, one that was in the corner of the top floor of the academic building. Nonetheless, she was nowhere to be seen.

Where the fuck did she go?

I moved to different sections and finally spotted her in the historical lane. Standing in the opposite aisle from hers, I watched the back of her head leaning against the shelf. She was sitting with headphones on and a book in her lap.

I stood there, making myself a part of the nothingness she finds her solace in.

I watched her. Secretly. Silently. Psychotically.

She started humming a tune I was not familiar with. The voice whispered from her lips, surprisingly, a newfound obsession to me.

She sings.

I closed my eyes, leaning on the bookshelf opposite the one she was sitting against, and heard her. Her voice was like a siren, devastatingly beautiful and damn right addictive.

She stopped. *No, fuck, sing!!*

"Hello." Was she on a phone call?

A long pause.

"I am alright, Dad. I am sitting in the library, away from everyone... No, I didn't hurt those who don't deserve it... No, it means nothing."

I understood the deserving part, and as she continued to speak, her voice turned heavy. Her words choked out, and it took everything in me from going there to her and making her fucking stop it.

She cannot cry, not without my permission. Nothing is important enough to need her attention other than what's related to me. And I've yet to make her break for hurting my father.

"I am alright... Dad... I miss Mom... I am sorry, I miss her." She started crying, and an unwanted hollowness created a hole inside of me.

Fuck, Chipmunk, don't cry.

"Chipmunk," I faced the other side, leaning on the same shelf she was sitting against on the different side of the aisle.

"What are you doing here?!" she screeched, and I didn't appreciate it, but I let it go—just this time.

"You're crying without my permission," I informed, ready to hear her rebel.

"Oh, now I need to have your permission for fucking crying?" She yelled in a low voice, sniffling hard.

"I can overlook it this time." I wasn't supposed to smile, but I did, and a warm fuzziness spread inside my stomach, crawling up my chest.

"Jesus, thank you so much, Treyton Spade. Your benevolence will be remembered throughout my coming generation." She snapped, but I liked that she wasn't crying like losing herself anymore.

"Did you like sucking my cock, Chipmunk?" I smirked, waiting for her little anarchy to stumble out of her lips.

"Jesus, no. Never. I didn't get to have my virginity lost, and here you fucking forced out a blow job from me. I was on meds. And what you did is called-"

"Do not complete that sentence. I warn you." Anger flowed in my veins, a heated lava ready to erupt. She's fucking mine and doesn't get to complain about what I reward her with and punish her for.

"-Sexual-"

"I fucking said, do not complete it," I warned again, pressing my words in a high and sharp octave.

"-Assault-"

"Chipmunk!!" Growling, I marched to her aisle, stalking my way until standing in front of her.

She was sitting, and looked small unlike her usual self. She looked too small and vulnerable with her red cheeks, nose, and lips. Her face was a Van Gogh-worthy collection. Tears depicting a rain shower on the white canvas is hardly an insult from a business major.

She looked up at me, her small face like a little animal. Her hair was a mess, but other than that, she was intact. No hurt that

I could see.

"Your smart mouth talks a lot." I went on my knees in front of her and holding out both her arms, checked for any injury.

"What are you doing?" Confusion decorated her innocent face while I checked her ankle, moving it slightly to test for pain.

"Does it hurt anywhere?" My eyes trained on the skin of her neck, roaming carefully to inspect for any minor injury, but what caught my eyes were the earrings and necklace she wore. I bought that for her. The ruby set.

"I am alright, and I don't know why you think I am hurt. I am not. And don't stare; it's creepy." She snapped, moving further into the bookshelf as if it'd keep her safe from me. Nothing existed that would.

"Where are the other pieces of the set?" My eyes were trained on her plump red lips. I want to eat them.

"I stacked them in the back corner my closet to keep it safe. I don't want to lose it." Her eyes fluttered down, and a small blush crept over her cheeks. Was she embarrassed or shy?

I don't get her.

"I thought you hated me," her lips trembled, and my eyes couldn't move from that dark red haze of lust.

She was right. I hated her. I hated her so much that I could fuck her any moment like she is my whore, but here's the catch, despite that hate lies a seduction play underneath it. I'd punish her like a lover, and both of it doesn't seem comprehensive anymore. It should be the opposite, but it's not. I don't think I'll ever be able to switch it otherwise, however I want her or loathe her.

"Yes. I hate you so much so, I want to punish you." The depth in my voice and her eyes that seeped into my own with a determined challenge settled a crazy nerve underneath my skin.

"There is no aspect that says it's not mutual. I hated you from the very first day. You dishonoured my mother's piano by fucking that girl in my music room. And now you hate me for hurting your father. It stands mutual, fundamentally proven." The heated gaze fucked me up.

I grabbed her jaw, drawing her face closer as she went on her knees, not moving away her chestnut browns from mine for once. Her pouty lips remind me of a Chipmunk's face stuffed with sunflower seeds. Hers, although, would look good with my cock choking her.

"What if I say I am the one who burned your precious dead mother's piano?" My breath fanned her warm face, and those beautiful eyes dilated, getting bigger as realisation simmered inside.

"No. You're... You're lying. There's no way you'd do... I know you wouldn't." Tears lined the corners of her eyes, and I smiled, appreciating the agony.

"Then you don't know me, Chipmunk. I have done it and would do it again without hesitation. Doesn't it feel bad, how you couldn't do a thing? Do you feel helpless?" I couldn't control the monster that ripped out of me, and how it enjoyed, savouring every second of her pain.

A tear dropped from the corner of her eyes.

"Please... Please, Treyton, say you didn't. I beg you. Confess you're lying." She screamed, not caring that people who passed were giving us a side-eye.

"I did. Get a hang of the truth, and quit the drama already. It was a fucking piano and not your mother's grave." It came out harsh, and I didn't predict any of it.

"It had my mother's soul. It was more important, unlike you, who have both parents alive." She pushed me, standing up, and I followed.

"Forget not, I was nearly about to lose one because of you." I snapped, not liking how she didn't acknowledge her own doing.

"Yes, and I am sorry. I have said multiple times, and I repeat again, I am sorry. I didn't mean to hurt him, and it doesn't mean you'll torture me, Treyton. If I had things in my hand, I would've chosen to stab myself instead of him. If I knew things would turn out to be this messy, I just would've committed suicide. Anything but to hurt you."

"Please keep it down, you both, or walk out." The interruption from the librarian wasn't appreciated.

Lyric took that chance, collected her stuff on the ground, pushed past me, and ran out of the library.

If this was a movie, I think I wouldn't be chasing her, and some fate factor would play to make the pieces fall in place despite the reality's cruelty. Factually, it wasn't a movie. It's real life, our lives, tangled and intertwined, and not how we wanted it, keeps rolling out.

I'd never say I said nothing hurtful, but seeing my mother picturing a world without my father was the first time I saw fear in her eyes, and that fear started resonating in me. Something that never bothered us before, now did.

I followed Lyric, furious. She doesn't get to have the last word, not the way she did.

I spotted her in the silent corridor and hauled her by the arm inside an empty classroom, locking the doors behind me.

"Why are you doing this? Leave me alone." She pushed, stitching hurt in her eyes, hiding other emotions that surfaced.

"You know why. There's no explanation needed for my action."

She struggled to catch her breath, and took a step back in an attempt to run away from me. Unfortunately, even her bad luck wasn't on her side.

I stepped closer, crowding her space and she was locked between me and the closed door that wouldn't budge even if she tried hard.

"Now, Chipmunk. Let's talk. We've got a lot of talking to do." With my emphasis on having her in place, pressing my body against her and her into the door behind, I had her where I wanted—right in front of me, watching me. Just me in her glazing eyes of dripping chestnut honey.

"What do you need from me?" A deep, shaky sigh left her lips.

Fuck those lips.

"You. I want you. To have you as mine to destroy, to punish, and to own. I want you as mine." Those were the words I wanted to tell her differently after that kiss we had in the park. Something special was there, dancing in the air, on our skin, sinking in our breaths that evening. Something enchanting. But the very night, she destroyed what we could've had.

"Until when? Until when having me will satisfy you because I am tired. I am tired of running, being hated, and hating you. Yet I'll always keep hating you for what you did. You took something precious from me, and none of it you'll ever understand. You're bound to have your way, but a person like me is always forced to follow others. Because it's right, to people and for people, but then what about me, Treyton? Where am I? Don't I have a will? What am I in all of it?"

I reached out to her, cupping her face carefully. Her tears shred me apart. And it doesn't make sense. None of it does. Do I want this? Do I want to have this altercation going on between us? Why this constriction in my chest doesn't ease down, and why, it bothers me to keep her at an arms length? I don't understand what she is to me.

"That's what you will have to tell me, Chipmunk. For me, to make it easy and make sense to myself. You tried to kill my father, and there is no child unless given in a different circumstance, would want to seek something from the one who hurt their parents, and mine are very precious to me. They accept me for my monsters and love me for my sins. No one is born that privileged. So, you have to explain it to me and make it easier for us. What are you, a sin, a punishment, a redemption, or an atonement? What makes more sense, guilty for craving you or an unforgivable regret for letting you go?"

Her eyes locked in a trance with mine. I know it's wrong on so many levels. I leaned close and had to bend down for our faces to be in front of each other.

"What if I deny to have it your way? What if I don't want any of it?" The visible tickles of her warm breath kissed my lips.

I moved closer, an inch a second.

"Why are each of our words filled with more questions than an answer?"

Her hands spread across my pecs, and I moved another inch closer, this time close enough to touch her with my lips. Kiss her with my lips and punish her with my breath mixed with hers.

"Then let me end this one time with an answer. Let me atone for my sins. Have me for however long you want until I am proven innocent. And make sure you end this between us the moment I am free of all the allegations." She arranged her words so meticulously, leaving no room for argument, and I had none to counter with. *She won*. This time, she won.

Her eyes fluttered close, and my eyes fell on her as our lips connected and devoured each other, taking something of us the other owned.

Lips to lips, tongues battling for supremacy, and hands

holding close.

I don't know of her, but I was scared to open my eyes, terrified to release her from my hold, but hated every second of the tumultuous thoughts.

"Lyric, is that you?" Voice of a man. It's not her brother. Someone significant enough to have her push me and step away from my arm's reach.

Not a wise decision Chipmunk.

Her eyes trained on the one standing behind me. Taking a deep breath, I turned to observe the fucker.

"I never imagined it'd be you, here, like this with a boy and causing scandals." He smirked, climbing the stairs of the lecture hall to us.

Fuck me, why did I forget this campus' lecture halls are big arse rooms and have four-way openings, one in each corner?

As the guy neared, standing in front of us, I looked around, each of the sides of the stairs had seats and tables but nothing in the vicinity to burn a human in seclusion. What's the use of parading old money if they can't afford that?

"Ciro, I thought you wouldn't return until May or before the music festival. So good to see you back." Was she talking nicely to a fucking human, or am I hearing things? Did she ever talk with such politeness and no contempt to anyone on campus other than her brother or Music professor?

"Who is he, Chipmunk?" I had to unclench my jaw before I cracked a tooth, all because that bastard had the nerve to stare at her like that, and I was the one who had to act patient.

"My senior. Ciro Aydin. He's a well-known musician in the industry and given many hits and billboard tops. I debuted with him last year, and in a way, we are close too." Again, here comes the politeness I never heard. She fucking explained every detail worth not even a penny.

"Ciro Aydin, Music major. Nice to meet you..." He stretched his hand, bloody muscles protruding, unlike for a musician.

I took his hand for a quick shake, and the callous touch felt even weirder because no musician would have such rough hands; however, manly they're. Something about this guy doesn't settle in place.

"Treyton Spade. Joined this semester. Business major."

He gave a quick nod and focused his attention back on my girl. Fucker has some pretty Hazel eyes but wouldn't have for long, and the longer he'd stare, the farther I'll make it painful.

"Does Grayson know about this?" He had no right to inquire about her whereabouts.

"About me being pregnant with my boyfriend's baby? I guess not."

Confirmed, she is still there, in her right space of mind but the guy lost the colours from his face.

"That's a joke." He tried arranging a pathetic smile but failed.

"Baby boy, didn't I ask you to impregnate me the last time we had sex? So why is another guy telling me I am joking? Haven't we signed the master and slave contract, so shouldn't my sugar baby be looking out for me, especially now when I am sensitive? Am I paying for this?"

Help me.

I take back my words, I want-don't-want this girl.

CHAPTER TEN

"You're the girl he told me about."

She never talked to me... like ever. Still, I know her. Scarlett is Hunter Owen's girlfriend, and the guy makes no excuse to parade her in his arms. When she doesn't look, her admirers get uncomfortable because he starts looking at them.

I swear upon everything holy, those eyes stare at your soul most illegally. I am personally scared of them.

"I hope it's good or else my sugar baby will be punished." I stuffed my mouth full of strawberry pie. Happy, I sneaked some money from Grayson to treat myself because stress started accumulating, and that's not good for my musical soul.

"He did say she could tame Satan if they ever met. Oh my god, you slay girl." She laughed, and I ignored her. Girlfriend or not, she wasn't my sex buddy and was not giving me money or a nice head, so I won't be the one entertaining her.

I did let her talk, though, because I wasn't responding, so she could talk as much as she desired. The stage was hers to own.

"Hey love, your class ended early. I'll go get you your lunch." Hunter popped up from nowhere, but surprisingly, Treyton wasn't there with him.

"Aren't you scared he'd cheat on you?"

Her face distorted in the best proportion.

"No. Why would he?" She sounded unimpressed, and her eyes spoke with a level of disgust. As if I give a single fuck about a pretty girl with pretty chocolate honey eyes.

"I thought he was hooking up with Treyton since he called Hunter, his brawny whore the other day. I was eager to know who is the top and bottom in their dynamic, and if I could get a live porn video of guys fucking each other like rabid dogs on a vape." I finished my last bite and smiled wide.

Her face contorted and couldn't go back to what it was before. That's what happens to normies who try associating with me.

"Scarlett, where is my brawny whore and... Um, Chipmunk? Am I seeing you eating with someone normal today, or is it a dream... don't open your mouth to spit and pop the bubble of this flower view I have in front of me." Treyton waddled and dropped beside me, not letting me speak until he groaned and glared at me.

His eyes curve in half-moon when he gets pissed, and it's the same as the day he walked into my class and borrowed me to have a chat, as he lovingly put it.

"What is this wet stuff I am feeling, Chipmunk?" He smiled through gritted teeth.

Hunter joined us with Scarlett's tray filled with expensive meal in hand, and my eyes glued to the chocolate fudge he had included for his girl.

"Yesterday, you said you want me, and I said I belong to you, right? And even forgave you for sneaking inside my house and forcing a blow job from me, or maybe not, but that's the matter I don't want to solve right now." I looked at Treyton eagerly, the wheels in my mind turning. I have not, and there is a completely different story for how I'll deal with that humiliation, but for now, I want something from him, and I'll get it in my way or highway, whatever works.

"And what the fuck does it have to do anything with the wetness I am feeling on my fucking bottom?" He growled.

Unapologetic bastard.

"That means, I am your girlfriend or so that's what normies call this transaction we've."

"I am damn sure a non-con blow job and biting each other with words doesn't mean girlfriend and boyfriend. Not in a normal dictionary." Disbelief dusted Hunter's face. In order to not show his discomfort, he covered his face with his hands.

It doesn't matter to me that his girlfriend looks at me as if I have a loose screw or how he judges me as if he's the messenger of God and my existence is unappreciated.

"No worries, I have Oxford. I'll look at it later. Now, Treyton, the wetness beneath you is called strawberry syrup. I didn't want anyone to sit beside me, so I intentionally dropped it there. You didn't heed my words, asked me not to pop your bubble and the beautiful wet mark on your pants would look like you just had your first period of life. Congratulations. What would you like to use, pads or tampons?" I grinned, so glad he sat there.

"Chipmunk." He rubbed his face multiple times with his hands, covering his expression.

I wonder what it'd look like.

"And now that I am your girlfriend, can you go and buy me a chocolate fudge? Hunter did too, and it's your turn to be a good boyfriend." I was at the epitome of my funny drugs because since morning, I had to deal with three constant bullies, and this was my only way of secreting happy hormones.

Yesterday, when I had to leave with Ciro to talk about a new music video, leaving behind an angry Treyton after calming Ciro from losing his shit with my pregnancy card, I was already planning hell for him. It was funny in its own way.

"Hunter, I like her already. No, maybe I am in love with her." Scarlett exclaimed, bursting into hysterical laughter.

I clicked my tongue, flicking a piece of hair from my ponytail and winking at the lady. "What to do? I know I am charming. Sorry, Hunter, ain't my fault your girl fell for me. And don't go thinking, you are inferior, just maybe, you can be born again to be Lyric Kensley."

He popped the fries in his mouth, shaking his head constantly in disbelief. Laughing with his girlfriend. For a moment, my focus shifted from Treyton. When I looked back to see why he wasn't speaking, I had to fix my sight anywhere but him.

Addictive whiskeys were staring at me, and the delectable shine in them, the dark hunger that lurked, wasn't supposed to send me part panic mode and part expectations.

I don't know what I was expecting because this was the very man who wanted to punish me for my sin.

"Treyton, stop being a creeper. You can look at her after changing. I'll have one of my men bring in a change of clothes for you. Go." Hunter emphasised, and Treyton glared at him, picking up the ketchup bottle and squeezing it on his burger. Bloody bully.

For a second, I saw the dark flash in Hunter's eyes, but it vanished somewhere and tipped into a soothing curve when Scarlett laughed at Treyton's childish behaviour.

Anyone could see how her existence affected him. There's a saying that Majesty, my brother's best friend, told me once. One day, it's going to feel special just to know you matter even when you don't realise, that you'll be a prince charming's charming smile. I don't know what she meant, and I may never know, but deep down, the way Hunter has these soul-reading eyes that soothe only by mentioning Scarlett turns me greedy for the same. Those eyes are what I've seen in my father's gaze for my mother, and I always thought one has to get married and spend years to achieve that.

Not true.

A janitor came, cleaned the seat, and Treyton returned, inspecting for any pending disaster waiting for him before settling down beside me. I quickly glanced at his white shirt, black jeans, and boots, and he looked hot. Mouthwatering, sexy, and a treat for sore eyes. His gorgeous blonde wavy curls were in disarray, and his muscles stuck to the fabric of his shirt. And fuck no, he had nice eyes, lashes too, and something else... *Cheating.*

Scarlett was done with her lunch, so I didn't suggest getting a chocolate fudge again and calling him my boyfriend because, give or take, I got my laugh, and it's not good to have someone else pay for your meals. I already owe Treyton a lot, already.

"You guys can carry on, I have to meet someone. I'll leave. And from next time, ignore me if you see me alone." The last segment wasn't a joke in my good year speech.

I walked away without meeting Treyton's eyes. The only feat I achieved in the small seconds until I was out of the cafeteria.

Despite feeling sore in every inch of my body, I still pulled myself together. I am sure by tonight, I'll be crying and shouting in my bathroom.

I feel my period is on its way, and the sore symptoms are just the beginning of a long hell in the coming week.

"Majesty," I shouted. She was together with her friends.

"What's future Duchess of Hastings doing with peasants?" I smiled, and she crackled, and so did her friends.

Majesty Hastings, as the name suggests, is related to British Royalty. Her parents are the current Dutch and Duchess of Edinburgh. I don't know for how long the Royalty will last, but I assume her cousin wouldn't get the chance to inherit the throne until he assassinates the entire army of the royal Windsor family.

And no offense to who can fucking hear my thoughts, but I assume it may happen shortly. I could see that coming.

"I could hardly catch up with your idiot brother and you. Care to tell me what he's up to these days? I just returned from my Grandmaster match from America, and the least he could do was come and greet his childhood friend. Bastard." She snorted at the thought of my brother and clued me in; she doesn't know about the recent events of the fifteenth. Given that she is a Grandmaster and one of the most stunning chess players I've ever come across, I understand if she's too busy to spend time on news and gossip sites.

Grayson never managed to beat her at the game, and I'll never forget how his ego ended up making them the closest of friends. At least that's what they told me.

Majesty is precious to him and me in a way, we nearly consider her family, if not anything more.

"Aglais and Everleigh, I'll catch up with you two tonight on the call. I'll leave with Lyric and find Gray's arse to whip and fix." She instantly sensed my discomfort and excusing, dragged me along with her.

We came to the ground, sitting on the bleachers as the football team got ready for their practice session.

I spotted Scarlett at the corner, sitting next to Treyton. While Hunter, whom I spotted on the field, was warming up.

I don't want to make any friends or enemies at this messed up point of my life.

"Is it just me or that hot guy beside Scarlett Willow is constantly staring at us? For the fact, I never met him so, is it you, Lyric?"

I stole a glance, observing how right she was. He did observe me, making every second so obvious it raised my concerns.

"I don't know what you're talking about. And don't you want to have your hands on the gossip in town? You're forgetting that the fifteenth of this month has just passed." That took her attention where I wanted, and it was away from Treyton's addictive whiskeys on me.

Don't fucking look at me with those eyes.

"Shoot."

I started telling her the entire story, downright to the point, about Treyton's father and everything without missing, except what Treyton and I had been involving ourselves in.

"Oh. My. Fucking. God. Lyric, tell me it's a lie."

"I wish it was. Grayson is putting off the fire for me, and that's where he is busy nowadays. But I am scared, Majesty. Whatever keeps happening scares me. I never thought, when I was waiting for this shenanigan to end my life, someone else's would be endangered. I am a burden, Majesty." Maybe it was something in my dull tone, but listening to me made Majesty-the-crybaby cry harder.

She can cry over anything, I swear. One wouldn't even understand when she cries on kitten meowing because Aglais, her friend, would lose her kitten's toy.

Typical sensitive Majesty. Only she knows why she cries other than my brother, who knows her like the back of his hand.

"Is everything alright, girls?" The musical voice chose that very chaotic moment for anarchy.

"Who are you?" Majesty yelled at him, hugging me tight and crying louder. There goes my plan to be discreet. Every watchful eyes were on us, and it looked promising how word of mouth would weave great gossips.

"Treyton Spade." He introduced, too confidently unlike my withering self.

Thanks to you, I'll have to beg this crybaby to shut her mouth in front of my brother, to whom she speaks like a chatterbox on drugs.

"Why are you here? Are you going to bully Lyric for stabbing your father?" She hiccupped, yet with ease, spelled her concern to the man who stared at me unapologetically again.

What's his deal?

"No. Surprisingly, I am here to deliver her chocolate fudge. She didn't have lunch and is pregnant with my baby." He smirked, and Majesty choked on air, eyes wide and face contorted to a masterpiece of disaster.

She turned to me so quickly, risking a whiplash, I was concerned for a minute for her jugular being hurt magically. That would've cost my brother a dramatic friend.

I knew Treyton was getting back at me for yesterday's episode where Ciro judged him. Our eyes were on each other, vehemently sparking with my bubbling anger and his smug smile.

"You're pregnant. Holy shit, I have to tell this to Grayson!!"

"Hold your fucking horses. I am not pregnant." I grabbed on to Majesty, who was about to make a run to my brother.

I glared at Treyton, enjoying this confusion, and sadly, it would've been enjoyable if not for Majesty being the listener. She makes everything dramatic and gives a twisted turn in her smart head. For the world, she would be a Grandmaster chess player, but for us, who know her intimately, she's nothing but a sleeping Karen who loves giving anything every meaning under the umbrella, whether it exists or not. Her soul must've been a film script writer in her past life.

"Then why is he here with a fudge, and how does he know you? Why does he know you? How close are you to playing a shitty prank on each other?"

Before I had the chance to retaliate her shit Sherlock questions, Treyton leaned and captured my lips in an endearing kiss.

I froze. Completely.

He nipped on my bottom lip, and a sweet, reluctant moan wheezed out of me. His tongue danced on the seam of my lips, fingers sensually running over my exposed arm until it dawned, he was fucking up with me.

I tried pushing him to no avail. He refused to leave me or

my lips and wrapped his hand around my throat, squeezing it. I couldn't push him back; partly, my brain stopped functioning from being choked and partly because there was a lingering tease in his touch.

He was kissing me with his lips, stealing my elaborated breath, not giving a fuck about the onlookers, and unknown to how much these confused and mixed feelings for him kept the push and pull vibrant in my head, runs chaos in my heart. *What is he for me, my hate, or my growing obsession?*

I could hear the loud gasps, but it didn't faze me because his tongue, playfully swirling on the roof of my mouth, was teasing me too much.

I wanted more from him. Expecting something when he abruptly pulled away and licked his lips as I panted. This was too quick, tortured, and detached for some reason for a kiss he has given me till now, and I could count them on my fingers altogether. Three times. Two passionate, and this one is nothing but a teaser.

His face was still close to me, his lips grazing my cheek, and I sensed them moving on my ears. His breath, without slithering on my skin, burning me, rhetorically elapsing, had a fine taste of an old sizzle, I only know of, have heard, but never knew how it felt. Fine as wine and dirty as the deed done.

"Tonight is an event, and I am sure you'll be there. Come wearing the dress I got you, clad in the jewellery set, and wear nothing underneath it. You follow me until proven innocent." He whispered in my ear for me to listen and, taking his exit, left a baffled Majesty, covering her mouth with both of her hands and her expression shouting, *'What the fuck just happened?'*

"It appears I am about to keep a secret from my buddy, Grayson, to save your arse for the first time in my long life." At least she gets the assignment.

I looked in my lap, never knowing when he slipped the cold cup in my hands. However, the chocolate fudge... *He remembered.*

CHAPTER ELEVEN

It was hurting.

Pain. Anguish. In line with this spectrum I had gone through, there stands no scale to measure my endless suffering. Somewhere, I had simply come to terms with it.

"Take care, and don't forget the medicine." Grayson's voice behind me resonated in the thin air.

The cold gush kissing my face would be touching his skin, too.

"I'll remember, now, please leave." My relationship with my brother was one that I cherished the most. Any remnants of it didn't last after the night of the most exaggerated accident. A glimmer of hope in me died that night, too, and what could I be presumably hoping for if the base of the wish is as unstable as my life going forward?

Ciro told me today to prepare for a new song, and on normal days, there was a chance I could. After three songs so far since my debut in the industry, I was growing steadily until the very scandal of that night blowing up the media and internet. What would be the outcome? I don't know, but my career will face some kind of backlash, and that's given.

Loneliness comes with a great amount of despair and anxiety. For this very reason, I hate being home alone. Dissolving in the crowd and becoming nothing helps me follow the life I want. The fair factor exists no more because everyone is there in every corner to ruin my day. I never knew what bullies were capable of until it started happening to me. They're petty and, for very vague reasons, don't like to configure why they should hate a person. If the idea satisfies them, the reasons and logic behind doesn't matter.

Rubbing my arms, I took a long sigh, wincing with every detail of the ominous night where I stabbed Treyton's father running through my head.

When I heard he was awake, I went to meet him in the hospital, hoping Treyton wouldn't come to know and my visit could stay as discreet as possible. Failure awaited in the path with no remorse whatsoever.

Treyton's mother, Lavender, just as beautiful as her name and warm to look at, met me before I could meet David.

I knew straight up I'd never get to apologise for my sin to the actual victim because she, who seems so elegant and composed for her public image, lashed at me. She hated me, and the vivid emotions orbited the second her eyes met my presence.

What hurt wasn't her insults but her tears and that shaky voice of hers where the trauma of the possibility of losing her husband was sown too deep, and it happened because of me.

I hated to be that person, causing someone to feel the pain of losing their loved ones, when I know the most, among a lot, how hollow a life becomes after they're gone. Every minute, second, and hour mocks you for being useless and incapable. It's filled with regrets, naive thoughts, and a whole lot of everything not suitable because grief may occur in five stages, but losing that very person comes with both the sense and knowledge of abandonment and a lifelong wound that'd never heal.

When Treyton told me how he loves both his parents, the flash of animosity in his eyes at the thought of seeing a life without either one of them plunged a dagger, digging deep inside my heart. I may not know why Treyton matters so much when we are anything but friends or acquaintances, but it was clear that I wanted to get rid of the title of his father's murderer.

If it begins with forgiving him for the piano, I will not. That's out of my power. What he burnt was the altar I worshipped on, twice.

Shivers entail with the very thought of the fire high in that room, snatching the idea of something precious to me. I wasn't there when it did happen. I don't know who was the one to refurbish the music room to make it look like nothing happened there, but what was gone was gone. My mother's piano turned into ashes.

I'd rather like to forget it if forgiveness isn't a part of it. As for what he did by coming into my room and forcing himself on me, I'll get back at him in one way or the other. I won't stand weak, and I promised this to my mom when we laid her in her resting place. However naive the me then was, the promise wouldn't change. If I've done something wrong, I'll own up to it. Otherwise, it's not my fault for what's happening to me.

Being scared doesn't change the truth; I am not at fault for others to come and find reasons to torture me. And I have nothing to lose because Mom told me in her teachings that'll live with me.

Her voice resonates to date, "always be scared of the greedy and the one who knows it all. One has nothing to risk, and the other has nothing stopping it."

In my case, I'm the greedy one. It's my greed to live like every normal person out there, free from the accusations, allegations, and people who find wrong in me, irrespective of the time of the day.

I won't let any negative thoughts conquer me. Not again. Not when I must remain as strong as the day I saw my father break into tears and my brother trying to self-harm. For them, I'll keep fighting, dreaming for a day when I'll have them back with me as a family, and even if that doesn't come by, I promise to smile and find my family that's made for me. Chosen by me. Because at the end of my journey, I want to look back at smiles and not regrets, and say 'that was a very beautiful life I lived.'

My mother, going inside the operating theatre, told my father she loved him. Kissed my brother's hand and mine and adored us with her drifting touches and eyes and the most beautiful smile that rested on her face when she said, "I'll be right back with your sister. Make sure you guys have everything at your disposal for the baby."

I have no regrets. Not when she was in the coffin, lying cold or beside my sister's grave, deep inside the soil.

I like to remember her last smile when I feel like everything is slipping from my hands. She left me with happy memories. I'll cherish them. She left me believing for a better tomorrow and I have to witness it with my own eyes.

"You would've hugged me, if you'd been here. I know it. I am your precious daughter, after all... But please don't be mad, I miss you a little here and there. I miss you when it's hard. I miss you on Mother's Day when I don't have anyone to return to or have a girl talk with. I miss you when I don't know how I'll introduce my boyfriend to Dad and Grayson. I miss you because I know you would've believed my lies. I miss you at the dinner table too, the food tastes bland without you. Still, thanks for being my mom, because they say I am pretty like you. That makes me happy."

"You're beautiful Chipmunk. More than your mom and she'll agree with me."

I jumped in my place, feline. Turned quickly and checked the broody shadow of the man I never thought would be here on my balcony.

The first time is a thrill. But the second time is a risk. Why was he willing to take that?

"Treyton?! Wait... What the fuck? Weren't you supposed to be at the party?" I got closer to him, standing at the corner next to the entrance of my room.

"That's not a nice way to welcome your boyfriend, Chipmunk. Not when he asked you something to do and you flat out rejected without a healthy negotiation. Communication is the key to a relationship." The fucker dared to mock me, and it's a petty act of strength.

"What fucking relationship and what boyfriend? When did that happen?" He was too much living in his head. The ego boost was speaking to the wrong nerve in his skull.

"Since today, when you claimed in front of everyone in the cafeteria, and I, in front of everyone present in the field. We're mutual, my darling." That smug smile, I'll use it to mop my house floor someday.

"Mutual, my arse." I spat, standing foot to foot with him. Who the fuck gave him protein powder when he was growing for him to grow this big?

"I'll take that arse any time of the day." *Oh, the smart mouth*. He tilted his head, running his gaze at the curve of my arse. Bastard.

Although, I took that time to look at him, and to my belief, I was right. He had on a suit, or at least he seemed to be contemplating it as his suit coat remained slung over his shoulder, and as I assumed, he wasn't a man who repeats a style. I always judged Treyton as someone who looks out for his appearance, and he did this time, too, pairing a crisp white t-shirt with the black suit and sneakers for a pesky casual look for the event. The rich bad boy that we commoners like to define it in our layman's terms.

As I was informed, it was a high-end, nice chitter-chatter kind of event instead of a formal one. Because my periods arrived and the heavy painkillers killed me with the pain, I could hardly step out of my room an hour before.

"No one is giving you. Why are you here and not at the event?" I was desperate to confirm.

"Stayed for ten minutes and saw your father and brother without you. So, I skipped the congratulatory dinner part and came." He shrugged as if it meant nothing. Wouldn't his parents be looking for him? What about them and others or anyone looking forward to meeting the Treyton Spade?

"Don't cook something in your small head, Chipmunk. Explain fast."

"I am on my periods. Happy?"

"No. What has it got anything to do with you not being there?"

I don't understand him. At one moment, he says he wants me, specifying that it's driven by the desire to punish me for my sin and causing him pain, but whatever he does has no connection with what he speaks of.

"I hope you're aware, your mother hates me. I see what can happen if she discovers your nightly visits and mingling with me. It's an invitation to disaster for both of us." I tried driving my point home, but he directed it to a highway that ended in a landfill.

"You overthink. Now, explain." His hands settled on my shoulder, giving a light squeeze, one that affirms me.

With a shaky breath, I told him why. "My periods are the most painful because of the medicines I take every day. Those pills have caused hormonal imbalance, and even if I addressed it with my doctor, she said I have to endure it. It's for my own good and my family."

His nose scrunched up, and brows drawn together.

"How are you feeling now?" The kind of concern that soothes me, and he knows it affects me.

"Better. I took some meds an hour ago. However, it'll not last long. After three hours, I'll feel tremendous pain all over again, and the cycle goes on. No give or take. I must endure."

"You don't have to be alone." The drop in his voice following the gushes of the air reducing to few decibels, the addictive whiskeys drinking me, mixed with his promise, stood so resolute.

"I don't understand. The more I think, the more you do something to humiliate me." Confused with him, that's the most prominent emotion other than the red haze of hate, anger, and the passionate lust that surrounds us.

"I will stay with you. You don't have to endure it alone, Chipmunk. I might not be able to do something with it, but I can promise to be there when it happens."

I took him up on his offer. I was running from my anguish and helplessness, and he chose to run with me for his own selfish reasons. Yet, all that matters is I have someone beside me to make it a little easier, a little less lonely, and a little endurable.

I don't know how I'll explain him to my father or brother but that's a later thought I don't want to entertain now.

"Who knew, the mighty Spade can cook." I giggled, sitting on the island while he stirred the soup pot.

When I brought him inside to show my house, looking at various rooms and photos from my childhood in the gallery of memories my mother and father built for Grayson and me, he complained he was hungry and asked if I had anything for dinner. My reply, 'I couldn't even swallow a morsel because of the pain.'

That's why Treyton was here in my kitchen, cooking for both of us. Searching online, which soup was better for periods and now, he was cooking two different types for me. Lentil and Chicken soup.

"Should I toast some bread, I like it with my soup."

He looked at me; his face was expressionless. "You wear my coat and sit where you're. I'll take care of the bread." He grumbled, handing me his coat dumped on the counter and went to the bakery basket to retrieve some bread for me.

Meanwhile, I wore his coat. It was warm. Engulfed in his scent, hugged by the fabric he wore felt like it was his embrace. It was cosy, and a fuzzy feeling settled in my stomach that hit me with a twisted churn from my impending cramps, too.

I focused on him, deviating my attention from the slow, simmering pain and breathing to control myself.

Treyton is fucking hot. His dishevelled blond hair, broad muscular back, and dominating height are picture perfect. I want to be fucked by him, and I blame it on my hormones.

"Soup is ready, have it with your bread." He served for both of us in small bowls, shaking my attention from him.

Two soups in one serving? I don't even eat that much.

I raised my brows, glaring at the bowls as he joined me on the island. We sat facing each other.

"Eat."

"I will but how am I supposed to eat everything? I don't eat much." My statement made him angry. I promise, his nerves popped on his temple. So very angry.

"Eating too little has caused you to suffer so *much*. Everything you eat should go somewhere, and I cannot see where it is going other than your small breasts."

"Fuck you. I don't have small breasts. Compared to my body, they look huge. You have small breasts, not me." I realised later what I said, and he was laughing.

"That's what I am saying. Your body shouldn't look small compared to your breasts. Eat and fatten up so I'll have some meat to hold on to when I fuck you, my little Chipmunk. I don't want you fainting mid-way." The tease in his voice, the addictive whiskeys sipping my sight, the lingering sparks in the air, I don't know if he was feeling the same. The haze was growing thicker day by day. It was not supposed to happen.

I fluttered my lashes, focusing on the food, and the first bite shut me up completely. Many people moan in delight, and then there is me who shuts her mouth in complete awe, devouring the delicious taste on her tongue.

"Are you blushing, Chipmunk?" That expression forced me to swallow my food in haste and not look at him as I gobbled up.

Yes, I blush. It is inherent in my family. If we like a meal or anything that excites us, our cheeks would warm up and glow red. Dad looks cute doing that, and Grayson looks pathetic. Mom looked noble, like a goddess, and as for me, I never want to hear it.

"Your cheeks puff. You do look like my Chipmunk. Should I bite those cheeks, have a taste of them?" He teased, grinning wide.

I pouted, now angry. He enjoyed my reaction and took on himself to tease the hell out of me.

"Shut the fuck up, and eat," I growled.

"Make me." He challenged.

And I just did that. Taking the carrot kept in the vegetable basket, I stuffed it in his mouth and his eyes widened. Smirking, I continued eating. Enjoying him grumbling and shooting daggers at me.

"You'll pay." He warned.

"I have no money." I retorted, appreciating the thought that he believed I was a rich individual.

Finished, we washed our plates, kept the remaining soup in the fridge, and walked out of the kitchen, aiming to move to my room.

We were around the corner of the stairs when cluttering sounds halted us.

Sharing a look with Treyton, my initial thoughts were about my brother and father, but it declined because Treyton switched on his phone and opened a surveillance application.

I was baffled. He had a camera at the party where his and my family were.

"Psycho," I whispered, and his smug smile grew feline.

Checking the different mini-screens, I spotted my father and brother in two different locations.

They were still at the event, so how come there was a voice upstairs on my father's floor?

In our mansion, my father used the first floor, and Grayson and I shared the second. At this time, if they were not here, no one should be. The guards are posted outside, and servants leave for their quarters in the evening. They'll not return if not called for.

"A thief?!" My eyes widened.

CHAPTER TWELVE

I was ready to sucker punch whoever it was, and the iron skillet Lyric was holding reminded me of a Disney movie.

"I will bitch slap the person with this, and then you hold them from behind. I know where the ropes are stored, so just for a moment hold the person for me, I'll tie the body and wrap the mouth with a cloth and then we can call the police."

Her master plan could go and fuck the pole. I have an intuition that it isn't a thief. Not what Chipmunk thinks, but the smile that decorates her lips and the shine in her eyes over the deliberate plan mapping in her little disastrous head looks fucking cute and makes me hard for her.

I want to devour this female alive, and at that too, I want to savour her like my first hungry bite.

"Don't zone out," she warned, tip-toeing in front of me. It was taking all the power in my body to fucking control when she trotted, her arse inviting me for first-row seats and those beautiful locks of hers flailing on her back. What would it be like, wrapping them around my fist and making her beg for my cock.

The urges are wild, salivating for one chance. However, she is the most clueless being who doesn't get my signals.

A fuck would do. It'd take me, the sinner, off her back. Just once, that's what I am asking for.

We reached close to the door behind which the noises were coming from. I had yet to take a tour of the first floor, and the picture we just walked past was her mom's. Covering an entire length of the wall, the smile resembles Lyric's, and her eyes are a carbon copy of hers and Grayson's.

She looked warm, holding her baby girl in her arms, her husband reading a book beside her, and her little boy sitting by her leg, playing with his toys. It was surreal that nothing about it was special, and despite the overall normal depiction, it was beautiful in its own way. The focus of the frame was her, in the middle, and I know why. She was the heart that kept this family alive, just like how my mother keeps our home bright and shining.

Maybe it was regret, or maybe I feel sorry for the piano I burned. Not now, but the dense feeling that the consequences will roll out in the future haunts a corner of my mind. It was bizarre; I never in my life regretted setting anything on fire, be it people, houses, or things, but a piano was making me picture the scenarios otherwise when I knew I'd do it again—fire is a part of me, anything that touches or comes in my vicinity would burn.

The question was, will I burn the world for this girl?

The clutter of violent noises and murmurs turned loud, making Lyric's grip on the skillet tight. She isn't scared to go in for another attempted murder. She's a natural, I can already tell.

"You said, the files were here," a man yelled, confident the residents were not home.

"That's not on me. You said we can find it here. This is our last chance, you idiot. Find it, or we've to resort to killing the man." Another aggressive bark. This time from a female and oh boy, was she angry.

I looked at Lyric and frowned, spotting her pale face. It only means she knows who is behind the doors.

Drawing close to her ear, I whispered from behind. My breath tickled her skin, and she visibly shivered. I liked my effect.

"You know who it is, Chipmunk?" My question received a

robotic nod.

Her hands were shaking, and I could see the tremors building from a deep-rooted fear.

Taking over the skillet from her hand, I intertwined our fingers, her in mine, small against big. Perfect fit. She looked at me, the fear shading her orbs, the cold sweat on her forehead now worrying me. Who the fuck is there to scare her so much?

The expression on her face bothers me.

"Eyes on me, Chipmunk." It was a command hardened with desperate aggression in my voice, one that wanted her submission but hated her fears submitting to another.

Her delicate flutter of lashes lined with my vision. Her chestnut orbs stared deep into mine, gauging comfort.

"Who?" I growled, waiting for her reply.

"Fuck. It's not here. Just kill Oberon Kensley." The raging shrills of the women, followed by a loud shatter of glass and thuds of heavy objects, took my attention. I couldn't understand what the heck was going on. Although, her words were enough to figure out what this mess and intrusion was about.

The thought that struck me abruptly pulled a horrific realisation into my being. If I hadn't been here, there were high chances Lyric could have been hurt in the altercation, given how it appeared.

I looked back at her; the ghost that she claims to see every night of the fifteenth loomed on her face, drifting in her lost eyes. She was shaking and forced to choose between tending to her or going after the two people inside this specific room, I made my decision.

Lyric is my priority.

Tugging her by the hand, I walked to the opposite side, crossed the corridor, and climbed the stairs to get to her room. She was following, but with her strange behaviour, there was a fine line between reality and her head that pulled her into the abyss.

Behind the closed doors of her room, I made her sit on the bed. Slowly, running my fingers through her hair, tucking them behind her ears.

In front of her, on my knees, I tried my best to level myself to her height.

"Chipmunk, are you there?" The tremors in her hand turned brutal. She suddenly looked at me, her pupils dilated, and heavy breathing raised my concerns.

"Trey-Treyton... They... My Dad... Kill... Lose..." She wasn't making sense. The panic attack was visible, and my eyes that turned to look at the pill bottle on the table immediately registered that this wouldn't be the one I'd resort to. Whatsoever happens.

When, as a child, I had been in and out of a psychologist's room, I met a lot of people. Some with anxiety and depression were among them, and the best I learned about were triple three.

But it would take a little more than that. I have to make it four or five.

"Chipmunk, can you hear me?" I traced her arms with light feather touches, and she slowly nodded.

"Tell me three things you see." Her eyes stared deep into mine; she was trying to control herself. With wobbling lips, she tried, and the effort was done for me. I could see that.

"Whiskey eyes. Moonlight. Treyton." I smiled hearing her, the common logic to separate my eyes and me as a whole. We will be talking about this soon.

"Tell me three things you can hear." Her breathing gradually turned a little slower compared to a minute before.

"Treyton. Wind. Crickets." I couldn't help smirking; now it was twice she took my name. Why was I so proud of it?

"Tell me three things you can speak about." Another wait. She was taking her time, gathering her senses a little at a time.

"Treyton. Dad. Kill." I hated how scared she was even to speak about the last two words.

I couldn't stop. She was coming back to me, and I needed her back, here with me.

"Tell me three things you can touch." Her once numb hands lifted in the air and clutched my shoulders, nails sinking deep and abrasing my skin through my shirt, leaving the imprint of her nails.

"Shirt. Treyton. Bed." Her pupils were normalising. I could see the warm gaze scratching on the surface of her haunted eyes. Given a different situation, she wouldn't let this pass without a snarky remark or a dirty joke.

"Tell me three things you can smell."

She linked me to her with her grasp.

I placed my hands on her thighs, rubbing my thumb on her smooth, milky skin. Letting her senses acknowledge I am here. She doesn't have to be alone.

"Treyton. Sweat. Tears." Smelling me was understandable, and her sweat was a prominent answer, but not the word tears. She wasn't crying, but she said she could smell them, which means she was chaining that emotion within her.

Her body, little by little, was becoming languid. Drawing her close, I took her lips in a searing kiss.

Sucking the plumpness until she gave in, responding to my touch, letting me have access to her mouth, and I jumped for the opening. Rolling my tongue and circling her mouth, clicking her teeth with mine, nipping her tongue, and devouring her not-so-innocent lips.

I want her. I need her. Right this moment. Right now.

Her hands snaked around my neck, fingers slipping into my hair, gripping for control.

She was falling and I fell with her.

I pushed her on the bed, never stopping the kiss. Her legs wrapped around my waist, the heels of her feet digging over my hips.

The long, endearing kiss halted when she was completely back in her senses and tried pushing me off her. Fucking cute, but there was no way I would let her go.

I let go of her lips, though, leaving us breathless.

"We cannot. I am on my periods." She whispered through her delicate, swollen lips, and I couldn't stop the smirk elevated on mine.

How fucking adorable of her to think, some blood could stop me from having her.

She's mine.

"You're my mess to handle, Chipmunk. However bloody it gets, I'll have you in any way. You're mine."

I silenced her with another deep kiss, and she moaned in my mouth when I pressed my cock against her pussy.

I trailed down, sucking and nipping her throat, licking my way farther down to her breasts.

Her nipples poked through the flimsy blouse. She was breathing hard, anticipating my touch, and I pressed the tip of my tongue on her right nipple over the blouse. She shivered, moaning. Her hands fell on either side of her, twisting the bedsheet beneath her hold.

Fucking adorable.

Sucking her nipple and taking a hungry bite of her flesh through her blouse, I left the wet cloth to harden the soft pebbles.

She was digging her nails and head into the mattress. Her back curved up, and her pussy humped me.

She wanted me, but not as much as I wanted her. My want was a borderline obsession—I fucking need her.

Groping her right breast, and torturing the nipple between my fingers, I went on giving attention to the other lady in waiting. Coming harder on her, eating her through my mouth and humping her.

"Ahh... Treyton... Please... " She cried, and I snickered with the notorious thought of being heard by the intruders.

With her eyes closed, and her chest rising and falling, the hunger intensified. I watched her tits brush against the fabric, and each time it did, she whimpered, biting her lips.

Tossing my shirt and removing my bottom clothing, I prepared myself, digging out a condom from the back pocket of my trousers and rolling it up my painfully growing cock. Once I made sure she wouldn't become pregnant, I helped her out of her pyjamas, and pushed her thighs, creating a wide space. The way she spreads her legs for me—fucking beautiful.

Her now-open eyes watched me, burning me under their innocent and trusting gaze.

"I won't go rough for your first time. Just enjoy, you're my priority tonight."

If sex is an art, I am an artist. I know what and how to play my game because it's not about just one person's pleasure.

She nodded, and I wrapped the dangling string from her weeping hole around my finger and slowly pulled it out. The blood-covered tampon in my hold made her blush in embarrassment. She bit her lip hard and curled her toes, digging her hips into the mattress. Her eyes turned to the other side, hiding from my gaze.

The dim orange and yellow lights of her room cast a golden glow on her smooth skin.

"Eyes on me, Chipmunk," I growled, pulling her closer by her ankle.

"I am sorry." She bit her lip again, and I fumed. My woman doesn't say fucking sorry, not for fucking menstruating—something that is a part of her.

"Sorry for what, Chipmunk? For bleeding, that is a part of you? Because that doesn't disgust me. Anything about you is important to me. It is my obsession. You get it. Do not be embarrassed for being you." I vehemently expressed each of my words that made her nod quickly.

Dumping the tampon over my t-shirt on the floor to keep the bloody mess minimum, I returned to her, holding her thighs and lifting her mid-air.

Inch by inch, I eased in her, letting the soft muscles wrap around me.

"Oh... God... Treyton." She moaned. The bloody mess of her hot heat and blood welcoming me easily with a loud squelch.

"Good. Chipmunk. Cry out for me, for your God." I growled, clenching my jaw and moving. The tears in her eyes rimming her lids made her all the more adorable.

I thrusted painfully slow.

"Treyton-Ahhhh... Fast..."

I pushed harder inside her, moving fast and thrusting fast, owning her with every inch I took of her.

Letting go of her thighs, I bunched her knees up to the middle section of her stomach and pushed my cock deep, taking her much deeper than before.

Her hands clutched my shoulders, her nails digging deep, and I gladly took her breasts in my mouth, nipping and sucking, switching between both before releasing with a pop and rotating my hips at different angles to find her sweet spots.

Biting and sucking her delicate throat and leaving my marks in a beautiful angry red and purple bruises, I hit a particular spot and smiled to realise that's what I was looking for. Her g-spot.

"More. Treyton, Oh... God... Please." She cried.

"Kiss me, Chipmunk," I panted, and she slithered her hands in my hair like a seductive vixen, drawing herself close and locking her lips with mine.

"More... Right there... Yes... Ahhhh." She moaned in my mouth, and I thrust repeatedly at the same angle, stimulating her at that spot, and with a scream, she came undone, collapsing in the middle of kissing me. The tears marked her face, and our saliva dripped from the corner of her mouth.

Something about this was erotic, and that made me want to go further, but given the blissful satisfaction on her face, I had to pull out.

Discarding the condom on the floor and pumping myself, I moaned and came all over her. Her face, breasts, and pussy were drenched.

She looked gorgeous, dripping in my cum.

"Thank you," she whispered, and I loved the sound of great contentment and sincere gratitude.

Now...

One is not enough with her. I needed more of her. Own every inch of her. Not just for tonight or for tomorrow but forever.

Looking at her like that hardened my cock again, but this was as far as I could allow myself today.

One evident truth despite my restraint. She is mine for taking.

I picked her up in my arms and went inside the bathroom, keeping her down in the bathtub and turning the hand shower on. The crimson water, a mix of red with her blood, cum, and clot, drained and looking at it, she smiled.

"What's that for?" I observed her, while lathering the shampoo and massaging her head.

"You're taking care of me after sex. I wrote that clause in the agreement."

I grinned.

"So, did your sugar baby performed well, Chipmunk?" The mere talk of stupidity amuses me. The words that'd entail after compels me to keep talking to her. Communication between us is no problem.

"Yes, but he can do better. Some practice would be needed. Still, I tell you, he's a good fuck and a caring sugar baby." Her smile... I loved it. The easiness in her tone and to have her back to the girl I know, it was rewarding.

I would burn the fucking world, turn it into ashes just to keep her the way I know, and that's her, existing as herself.

"He sounds like a great guy. I wouldn't mind sharing him with you." I mused, engaging the conversation because I wanted to lead it somewhere.

"Don't you dare? He belongs to me." She turned over her shoulder, glaring playfully.

I cocked my brow, smirking. Coming from her mouth, the feral and territorial claim is sexy. "And you? Whom do you belong to, Chipmunk?"

She licked her lips, staring at her painted toes and nails, the one she got done with me. I should take her for another nail makeover.

Moving to scrub her, I squeezed the body wash smelling like candy and started lathering her body.

"I don't know. Do I even belong to anyone? Everyone hates me. When it was hard, I thought existing for myself was enough, but it wasn't. The past two years were the loneliest years of my life, and then you walked in, trampling whatever crossed your path. However, our dynamic was, be it enemies or strangers who liked each other's company in twisted ways, talking to you was easy. You made me crave something I don't know what to name, and I knew, maybe I could exist for you too, because you saw me. You didn't ignore me, and you matched up to my anarchy with an enthusiasm. Until hell broke loose and I ruined it all."

Her voice turned gloomy, and it ignited a burn inside my chest. It was scorching and coercive to have my beast scraping my surface again for a let out. To let go so he could slit anyone who made the siren he admired cry .

Within her beautiful voice, there existed an ugliest cry.

"What happened that day?"

She knew what I was talking about and winced at the mention of it. To date, I have yet to sit down and have a conversation with my father about the downfall of the fifteenth.

My mother hated any mention of that day, and my father's recovery gave me no choice but to push it on the back burner.

I need something of it. Any fragment to know if it's just me who thinks she did something awful or if there is a truth not registered and hidden in discretion.

"I don't want to talk about it." That was a straight,

unapologetic decline when I deserved more than bits and pieces.

"Then tell me, who are the people we heard talking like they fucking own this place in that room." My deep voice, one which she couldn't ignore, made her jittery. I need something to feed my hunger to know it all.

"It's my father's secretary, Henry, and my psychologist Jessica. I have no clue why they were here, but I know what they want. To kill my father." She huffed a shaky breath, mentioning about the episode.

"Are you scared?" I knew she was. There is a difference between knowing and hearing her confess.

I washed the soap off her, opened the faucet, and filled the tub with lukewarm water.

She took her time until I went to take a quick shower and returned to her. She was soaking and holding herself protectively.

"What if I choose to be scared? Who will protect me? I am alone, Treyton. I've done wrong to everyone. The least I could do in the name of favour to anyone is die silently. Be gone so no one would be bothered."

"Is ending your life all you think of?" This conversation was leading to doom. Her inner fear was poisoning her, conquering her in the worst way, and that, for the first fucking time, scared me.

The idea of losing someone who wasn't my family but seemed now to be the very extension of my existence.

"I never did before. Not until you burned my mother's piano. A faith in my life that kept me together from shattering."

I knew somewhere in me, I'd regret that decision and I was regretting it now.

The water that filled her tub, the small ripples in them bleeding back in the expanse, proved to be the very reason I knew for my upcoming action.

I walked to her cabinet below the sink and pulled out a blade from the razor.

"What are you doing?" Her eyes were horrified to see the blade in my hand.

"Sit where you're, and do not move until I say," I commanded. Wrath creasing my voice.

"That makes no sense, Treyton. What you-" I halted her abruptly, pushing her head down under the water, and she came up coughing.

Before any words could come forth, I slit my palm and dipped it into the tub filled with water.

"Treyton," she screamed, but holding her nape, I stopped her and made her watch the water turn red. "Treyton, please. What are you doing? It's scaring me." I made her watch the colour of the water turn a forbidden red.

Grabbing her by her hair, I forced her to look into my eyes as the red liquid covered her body.

"You need a faith then I am your faith. You need a God, then I am your God. I baptise you, Lyric Kensely, now live for me. Worship me, your only God." I dipped her back into the tub as she came up, and the crimson droplets cascaded from her head to her body. Water dripped and formed circles around her breasts.

She stood up, her eyes still on me as I drained the water and washed her again before putting her in bed.

She silently watched. There were no words between us to speak of, and there was no need for them.

She knew what I meant. I knew what I wanted.

CHAPTER THIRTEEN

I have long stopped counting my miserable days. Has long since stopped functioning as part of normal human society.

My faith disintegrated the day I lost my mother and her blessings, yet I earned a God who may have commanded me to follow his faith, but he is a God who worships me.

His addictive whiskeys have *me* in their beautiful reflection. Show my face in their reflection. Still, I am scared to put a word to it.

"Lyric Kensely." Grayson barged into my room, shouting, not considering knocking and showing some human manners. "Where is my white t-shirt and black pants?"

Why would I know that? Is he listening to himself?

"No, I do not and don't want to." I frowned.

He manages a diva's wardrobe for the sake of God. He can wear anything, whatever he wants. Is there any need to find missing clothes among his thousands of pieces?

"That's my favourite pair." He barked, and I clicked my tongue, annoying him.

"Yeah, you're the only one who has ten thousand favourite clothes." My snarky remark wasn't appreciated on his end.

He glared heatedly, pinning me under his gaze, and marched inside my walk-in closet to look for his yet another missing favourite t-shirt.

"Where did you hide it?" He growled, rummaging through my clothes.

I tapped my nails on the wall, waiting for him to be over with this nuisance. What are we, two, to keep playing the thief blame game for clothes?

"In the drawer where my bra and knickers are kept."

He opened the drawer, rolling his eyes and growled in fury, unable to find it.

"It's not here." Someone was furious.

"I know, right? That's what I was trying to fucking tell, it's not here. You need to get a hold of yourself and act your age, Grayson. Why would I steal your clothes? Who are you, my boyfriend and us wearing each other's favourite picks are couple goals?"

"Thank God we are not or else, my love life would be doomed." The man has a mouth on him.

"It already is." I turned, stepping back into my bedroom, and he followed. Grumbling under his breath how much he hated me. That's a sibling hate voice, I am well aware of.

"Was someone there last night in the house?"

Don't go there...

I panicked for the worst and horrible reasons. Yes, there were people, or shall I say, intruders in our house last night, but everyone came for different reasons. One took my virginity and faith from me, and the others are plotting to take my dad.

One was successful in getting what he wanted, and the others left empty-handed.

"I don't know what you intend to refer to. I still have no clue where your clothes are or who was here last night." Lies straight through my teeth.

Now thinking back, Treyton, before leaving me, did change into a new piece because his were ruined with my blood.

The psycho was wearing my brother's clothes. Shit!!

"My conundrum made you sweat, isn't it Lyric?" I hate that he was so keen. The way he smartly reads a person through their voices, both I hate and love about him.

"I am hungry. And later, I am going shopping with Majesty." I informed, rushing out and trying to wipe away the cold sweat on my neck.

"Did you take your pills?" That question halted me. I swayed through the night and morning with my head filled with Henry and Jessica. Their conversation was on repeat, and every time the panic rolled in, my sore waist would keep me grounded.

"No. I will not be taking them ever again." I should've known better than to use that tone with him. Grayson could be OK with a lot of tantrums, but what he hates the most is someone keeping him in the dark as if his opinions and consent don't matter. He hates to hand over his authority to anyone.

"I am not going over the pill discussion again, you hear me, Lyric? Go and take your pills right now before I shove it down your throat." He was pissed, and if I try to reason with him, he'll say, I am making stories again.

I want to know more about Henry and Jessica's plan and how they will move forward. I want to protect Dad at any cost, but the only way to do that is to keep acting mad.

"Fine. Don't boss me."

Taking the bottle from my bedside table, I tossed two pills in my mouth and crushed it...

Yummy?!

The realisation simmered inside as I kept chewing the pill and swallowed. It was not my regular pills prescribed by Jessica, but chocolate candy in blue that resembles it. Who did that?

Only one person could've.

I couldn't help but smile to myself, chuckling at the bottle, as I grabbed the glass of water Grayson passed me and took a big gulp.

"That expression is for?" He cocked his brow decisively.

I shrugged and followed him out of the room to have breakfast with Dad.

"Not everything is for you to know, get a life for yourself... Oh, I forgot you've none." I winked, and his piercing orbs, a resemblance of mine, creased on the corner with fine, impenetrable lines of scepticism, fading into his rugged contour that females fall for. He's got a mole right under the corner of his left eye, just like Dad, and a dimple that only shows up when he clenches his jaw or smiles.

My brother was not just a golden boy by name or lineage. His appearance is an entity of a deity of war. Despite the toned and muscled edges, and lovely ivory skin tanned from vigorous physical exertion of power, he is still my brother who shares the colour of my eye, hair, and skin. Has the same blood as me. I don't care if it was not purely melted monochromatically as my soul. He is my only brother.

"Good morning to both of you." Dad's voice settled my nervous heart, suppressing its cry.

I was on edge and helpless with every intricate knowledge of my father's secretary and his girlfriend plotting against him, betraying the trust he put in them. Letting one carry out his power and the other heal his daughter.

My dad doesn't hate me; I hope so. And I also hope neither does my brother or Treyton. A girl can only put out her wishes in the universe.

"You look much brighter today, Lyric. Medicine and sessions with Jessica are finally showing their signs." He smiled, patting my head for the first time in forever, and took his place over the head seat.

I stood perplexed, stroking the spot he touched. My heart felt frenzy and the fuzzy feeling made my lips wobble.

Why was there an exhilaration inside me? However, I was aware of how it made me feel.

"Is there a problem, Lyric?" Grayson sat by my father's side, and I took my place opposite to him.

"Dad, would you mind giving me some money, I am going shopping with Majesty," I informed him.

Majesty wanted to visit the same salon where I had my nails done, and I didn't want to come out to her as some neglected child who couldn't even afford a glass of water if she mistakenly stepped into a diner. True, though. The apple of my situation doesn't fall far from the tree of reality.

"I will gladly, Lyric. Mind me asking, where did your money go?" Dad's eyes struck me as unapproachable dynamite.

"The monthly allowance that you provide me and the money I earn from my recitals, is that what you're talking about?" Way to go, Lyric. He'd think you are dumb if he didn't, yet.

"Wisely, if we both are referring to the same subject."

My eyes drifted from him to Grayson, and he cocked his brow, annoyed. His eyes speaking, *'What?! Why are you looking at me like that?'*

Biting my bottom lip, I stared back at Dad, consolidating my spine to come forth with a viable argument. I don't wish to offend anyone.

"Since the day, Jessica diagnosed me, you know that Grayson is managing my finances. I don't have any authority left over my money after that happened. I have no money on me."

The perplexed expression on Dad's face was an understatement. It evapourated and left wrath, etching the fine wrinkles on his gorgeous face.

"What am I hearing, Grayson Kensley? Did you scam your sister?" Dad was furious. I could see his disbelief shredding his trust in my brother.

Sometimes, even I am forced to think whether my brother means his actions or if I fail to understand him.

"No. This little bitch is framing me." Grayson yelled, his eyes meeting my father's, and both the males appeared deadly.

"Henry told me that after speaking with Lyric in the past, she was the one who set up this arrangement. Letting you manage her finances. I know it's not a lie." Dad deadpanned.

"Wait a second, what finances? I don't know of any and I'm not managing any. Lyric, what's all this about? Why are you putting dirt on me?" Grayson accused me, taking it all in and punching the table as he stood up.

Dad's eyes were confused, and he judged me when he came to know Grayson's perspective. Of course, if he isn't managing my finances, then who'd other than me?

"Lyric, explain." Dad's demanding tone and the angry veins on Grayson's neck and hands coerced my naive brain. I started connecting the countless loopholes. At every answer, one person was in every one of them.

My family didn't abandon me. Henry made them do that. He painted me in front of them as an incapable-functioning adult while he leeched off my money behind our backs. How couldn't I see through his threads of lies when everything was right in front of me?

I put my trust in the man my father chose to accompany him and guide my brother in his absence.

"Sir, good morning." The interruption was caused by none other than Henry. I clicked my tongue, giving him a bombastic side-eye.

He walked on us at a terrifically perfect time. Angling his frameless glasses on his nose and sporting his workplace costume, a three-piece suit. Despite the gallant endeavour of a curt head bow to Dad and respectful nod towards my brother's way, his very presence was icky to me.

I was seeing him in a completely new light, and the dazzle of his venomous being was disgustingly bright.

"I sense tension, did I choose the wrong time for our rendezvous, sir." The fucker's inspecting eyes, I wanted to bitch slap.

"I wanted to confirm-"

"Yes, we wanted to confirm if the colour for our house renovation should be green-themed or pastels. Dad suggested a wooden design would be better and Grayson wants to see white. So, what do you think Henry, which theme suits?" Letting Henry on anything anymore means further danger, and I cannot let risk accompany us. He has enough information and is rotting his way into our lives. Any wrong move or he becomes alert could backfire.

He can hurt my dad or maybe my brother.

I cannot let anything happen to my family.

"White and woodwork would be lovely and maybe incorporating green would make a complete modern sophisticated theme. I hope that helped, young mistress."

I mirrored his smile, observing the way his eyes crinkled, while attempting to decipher the confused looks on the faces of the two individuals I preferred he kept his distance from.

Focusing my attention on the two important men in my life, I grinned wide, showcasing my Colgate smile.

"We are a family, and I know we'll make it on our own. The best decision for our affairs. I am thankful for Henry's opinion, but letting an outsider make crucial decisions for us wouldn't sound great or reflect nicely on our family." The point of me speaking like that was rather a crystal, shining in the eyes of the men who understood and disregarded their earlier decision to confront Henry to gauge out the truth of the mess we just discovered.

For once, they chose to believe their liar family member.

And... I need a plan. Fast.

CHAPTER FOURTEEN

The purring of the engine blasted as I moved in the dimly lit night from the street lamps, anchoring my body and cutting the breeze flowing across.

Riding my bike brought me relief. A preposterous control, hard to find in the loud noises of this world.

Life has always been a monotonous way of pre-planned checkpoints. One I had no allure towards.

Death never got to me like it did to the others. I had no new chapter exciting me or relations to look up to. And then, she happened.

Like a breath of fresh air, she was the meaning of anarchy that seduced my celibate life. Her presence was everything I searched for in this meaningless world.

The thrill surged in my veins and blended in the air, only to halt where I wasn't supposed to. The Mayor's mansion. Carved in pompous stones of money and attraction.

It was a tower, one that trapped the princess, and parked on the opposite street from the mansion, hidden from the eyes of the people, I waited for the very beauty to make her appearance. It was time. She's always there by ten, bathing in the moonlight and letting the fucking breeze play with her hair.

The silhouette appeared. The richness of night filmed her as she stepped by the railing and looked up in the sky.

I am always here, unknown to her, watching her looking at the moving clouds.

She speaks to her mother, now that I've come to know, makes all of it surreal and serene. A picture I am hungry for, and without knowing, I find myself here each night, waiting for her to appear.

Five minutes, that's all I get before she disappears, and I'm back on the road as if waking up from a dream.

She's a dream. One I'm not allowed to have.

The scrambling of metals and horns deviated my focus, and I saw her father driving out of the mansion.

A smirk tipped on the corner of my lips. Fucking perfect.

Crossing the road, I was back by the wall that had a tree on the opposite side, and I already had a hollow section previously engraved to ease my visit. Climbing over the wall and down the tree, I shuffled over to the mansion and stopped by the back gate leading to the kitchen.

None has caught me, and one who did was muted with the money.

Opening the door, I entered–

"Treyton?!"

–And halted.

What was she doing down here? Shouldn't she be in bed, sleeping?

I read her confused eyes, staring at me with a gaping mouth. Her little nothingness she calls pyjama is a fucking temptation, and it rattles on the chains I use to shut my monster inside.

"What are you doing here? My brother is home," She whispered, striding to me and pushing me out from the kitchen door, used by the staff and me.

Rolling my eyes, I picked her over my shoulder and dumped her on the kitchen island, parting her legs and standing in between.

She didn't speak a word, scared of her brother coming down, and this enunciation of forbidden hardened my cock to do the illicit.

"How have you been, Chipmunk? Missed me?" I stroked her thighs, loving the jolt that straightened her delicate spine and the goosebumps playing on her skin under my touch. It turns me fucking feral to have a taste.

"T-This i-is not a j-joke, Trey-Treyton. My brother will find out." She attempted to push my hands off her, but I gripped her tighter, hauling her close to me, wrapping her legs over my hips.

"Did you miss the ache between your legs? The taste of me on your lips?" I inched closer to her face with each syllable.

"Treyton," her voice trembled. Placing her hands over my shoulder, she tried pushing again to no avail.

"Kiss me, Chipmunk."

Her face twisted in a chaotic blend of shock and deep thought. She gnawed on her lower lip, and a rush of heat surged through me, igniting a wildfire in my groins.

Say yes, little anarchy.

"Leave after this." She bargained.

Her lusty eyes held me in a chokehold, and she descended cautiously, taking my lips between hers. I could taste chocolate fudge on her tongue, and my hunger rose.

Lost in the sensation, I cupped her face, forcing her small mouth open and plunging my tongue inside, devouring her mouth.

She was crumbling in my hold. Panting. And I fucking loved owning her. The deviant taste of her pushed my monster forward.

I pulled away, leaving us breathless and tortured.

"I missed you," she panted, her falling and rising chest inviting me to have my way with her, and I was going to have it. Have her tonight.

"Strip." I ordered.

She paled. Her eyes glared in horror.

I wanted nothing more than to put my throbbing cock between those lips and ram that warm cunt. My impatience was removing the shells of the facade.

"No." She deadpanned, and I couldn't help laughing at her innocent denial.

"Nice try, but you know... You want me. Just as much as I want you, Chipmunk."

She denied it, pushing me away, jumping off the island, and attempting to leave the kitchen, but I managed to grab hold of her hair, coiling her loose strands around my wrist and pulling her back to the island. I then gently bent her over the counter in an estimated flow.

"You're crazy, Treyton. Leave me. Anyone can walk on us." She thrashed, and I laughed.

The unhinged me out on the surface, tasting her fear in the air.

"You follow your God blindly and oblige him just as much. If your God wants you, you'll serve him yourself with gratitude." I growled in her ears, hooking my fingers in her shorts and knickers and sliding them down with ease.

She moved, backing from my hold and trying to run, and it made the hunger flare. I fucking wanted to feast on her.

"Treyton-Ahhh," she moaned when I slapped her arse.

"Thank you, My God. Only that should leave your lips." I stroked her pussy, and smiled, finding it drenched and welcoming.

"No. Fucking, leave me." She was retaliating, hearing the loud noises of her brother and his female friend fighting.

"I hate you, Grayson, fucking die."

"Don't force me to stab you to death, Majesty."

They were at each other's throats. None held back. I don't care and give no fucks either.

"Shhh...The louder you're, the more you invite the audience. And I'll not be stopping for anyone." My words affirmed her, and she stopped moving. "Good girl."

Grabbing a lemon from the vegetable basket, I sliced and pushed the wedge inside her mouth, gagging her. "Hands flat on the surface, and I'll only hear thank you. Do you get that?"

She nodded, and I released her from my hold, appreciating the submission.

Holding the wooden spatula from the opposite counter, I traced the bouncy curve of her small arse. Her muffled voice died in the loud background noise.

"It's sour." She winced.

"Good girls, accept." The wooden spatula ripping the air

struck her milky skin, and she arched her back, moaning and wincing. Her saliva dripping with the lemon juices from the corner of her mouth was inviting.

Leaning over, I grabbed her jaw, angling her to face me, and licked the corner of her mouth. Tasting the acidic liquid. Fucking. Sour.

"What should you say?" My eyes pierced hers, and she forced the words out of her lips.

"Thank you," the incomprehensible syllables wheezed repeatedly with each strike to her arse. Hit after hit.

Tears decorated her cheeks, and lemon juice mixed with her saliva smeared on her mouth.

She panted, spent and exhausted from the spanking. Now that her punishment was over, her reward awaited.

I walked to the fridge, picking the ice cube container, and returned to her. Placing one chilled cube on my tongue while stroking her clit from behind with my fingers as I went down on my knees and feasted on the weeping pussy, rewarding her for being my good girl.

She moaned loudly in ecstasy, my cold tongue plunging inside her warm hole and stroking deep. Her muscles spasmed, enveloping me, and I delved further, sucking her in a fast rhythm, while also adding in two of my fingers, stimulating her pleasure and teasing her clit right in front.

"Oh, God. Thank you." She screamed, wincing, and I kept stroking and rubbing on her sweet spots, reading the tremble in her legs as she climaxed on my tongue.

I sucked, dragging her orgasm.

Huffing, she rolled on her back, spitting the lemon wedge and spreading her shaking legs on the counter.

I stood between them, unzipping myself and tearing a condom from my teeth.

Her face was red, and the smile adorning her was the fucking reward I was hungry for.

Helping her out of her blouse, I admired the view and the anticipation in her eyes as she waited for me.

"Fuck me. Please." Her lips wobbled.

I smirked.

"Good girl. Swallow my cock inside that filthy cunt and moan the name of your God as he rewards you." I thrust, inching deeper and settling to the hilt. My relationship with her is unnamed, and I wasn't sure where to draw the line between me and her.

She held the edge of the counter above her head. Her entire body bounced with each thrust as I went deeper, taking my sweet time with her.

"Fuck me fast, preschooler at sex." She cried, and I bit her neck, angry.

"Don't fucking run your mouth." I drove deep, ramping up the speed, unleashing my primal instincts on her.

"Then fuck me like you know how to!" She sat up, holding my shoulders and moving her hips to my rhythm.

"That fucking mouth of yours," I groused, claiming her lips and pounding her vigorously. Who the fuck would say she was a virgin.

"Oh... God... Yes... I love it...Ahhh," she moaned, and I grunted, leaving her lips and sucking the column of her throat.

I went feral, pounding into her, and she climaxed, collapsing in my arms.

"Thank you, and pull out please, I am tired." Closing her eyes, she nudged her face in the crook of my neck.

I smirked. How innocent of her.

"I've yet to cum, Chipmunk, and once wouldn't be fair to me when you climaxed twice." I licked my lips, pounding her again, and she convulsed, her face upright, looking at me in horror.

"No. No. I'm tired." She complained, and I slapped her sore arse.

"Not so soon." And started pounding her again, and again, and again like an animal.

I reached my high and climaxed.

By the time I ended, she fainted in my arms, and I had to go and put her in bed.

"I knew something was off."

My tongue danced over my lips as I spun around, and there he was—Grayson, looming in the doorway of Lyric's room like a shadow come to life.

"What am I supposed to do?" I rolled my eyes, walking to the door, but he didn't budge.

"What do you want from my sister, bastard?" He glared, and I glanced over my shoulder to confirm Chipmunk was sleeping.

"Voice low. I'm not your minion, Grayson Kensley." I growled.

"Filthy like you would never be. Stay away from my sister." He warned, stepping back, and I pushed past him.

"Protect my girl, and if you fail. Remember. I. Will. Fucking. Kill. You. Brother or not."

I walked away, not bothering to entertain more of him.

CHAPTER FIFTEEN

There's only one way to help her. Talking to my father before I lose something precious from my grasp.

"There's one more way." Hunter's voice collided with my thoughts.

"Will you take money to carry on? Fucking speak." I was not taking his pauses as a gesture of attaining enlightenment. He was no saint.

"There's a very powerful secret society linked to one of our professors." He suggested, and my face gave away how disappointed I was with my whore.

"Suck my cock because that's the only thing that could make me ignore your pathetic remark. For once, I'll try to play for the same team."

He sipped his drink unbothered. I hate my whore. On occasions more than I ever did.

"Listen before speaking. That's what I hate about you, Treyton. You never listen, just fire off words like arrows you can't take back.."

"I am disappointed, my not-so-virgin priestess with a dick, using his tongue too much on me in every wrong meaning of the word. I need no lecture." He had to get this message from my tone because I wasn't in the mood to voice my thoughts.

"Humph... If it had been someone else, I wouldn't take a second before cutting their tongue and shoving it down their throat. Dance on privileges fucker; you are my cat with too many lives to keep on living after and after talking to me like that. Ignoring all my warnings." The dark sheen emanating from him would've scared anyone but not me. As he said, a truth in each word of his; I am the only fucker who was allowed to fuck with him and walk away with his head intact.

"What, want me to sit in your lap and give you the night of your life, you couldn't give your girlfriend? Try on someone else, not romantic to me." I smirked, and he crushed the coffee paper cup.

Schooling his dangerous features escaping the tomb of his dark lair, he carried on where he left off. "Omen, a secret society of cold-blooded murderers who enjoy the play of chase and hunt. Professor Nile Clifford is the leader and our wingman for us to get some answers." His expressionless face and my surprised one matched, I guess.

"He is my economics and maths professor. Are you sure that hot-as-hell rude guy behind glasses and books is a secret society leader?"

"I have no words. Did he cause an inferiority complex?"

"He has to be born a thousand times to deserve one word of praise, my whore. Girls in my class, a specific number of boys and Scarlett calls him Professor Daddy, and I only tried to sugarcoat their lusty words for you." I knew I had him where I wanted. Hunter is sensitive about Scarlett, and her praising and being on a kinky naming basis means Hunter, the dark lair boss, wasn't happy.

He'd help me, and not with the intention of friendship. It'd be the ideal image of wiping Nile Clifford's name from history.

I had to up my game a little in my favour.

"Come. We'll meet the motherfucker, now."

Why does the sound of heat and agony make me happy?

It wasn't entirely about his rugged-looking beast physique like an aged wine in a century-old chalice or how he doesn't have to speak to make it known, he was there in the room.

Nile Zale Clifford, age 32, a prodigy mathematician and multiple award winner of great theories, research works, and an advisor to many major companies, has his chokehold from the modus operandi he achieved that resonates with his unique civilised ethics not for many to understand.

Not to forget, he is one of the trustees of our college. A man of words, strict with procedures and commitment, out-of-the-box tactics, fine French cuisine enthusiast, and passionate about his numbers. The only few details I knew of him were from the class of society he operated in. The upper polished class of light and old money.

The only man who knew what he truly was, the real monster inside the old castle of night and winter, was sitting next to me, pissed to spot his lover sitting in the front row seat of the very man in question's lecture.

I can already see her demise coming. The taste of Hunter's wrath is lingering in the air.

To think what would be this time, Scarlett hung by the ceiling naked, and him spanking her with a crop or tied in a sailor's knot drooling on his cock. Both are the very experiences I hate to admit, I walked on and never was prepared for it. My damn habit of not knocking costs me everytime, but I still not learn.

I didn't sign up for my friend's sex coaching.

"That's all for today, if no one have any questions, you all may leave. Do not forget to hand over the assignments by next Monday. If you slack, say bye to your credits for this course and I'd never mind seeing you here with me for another year. And those who'll receive my email today, be ready to take the retest because you failed, and I'll make it hard so you can fail with flying colours, again."

Yes, that's his way of warning us as if it's some haunted movie with freaking messages and creepy dolls. How girls find him sexy, I have no clue. For me, he sounds sinister, and each time I attend his class, I breathe in the air, the psychotic drug mixed around him, one I am aware of. An air like mine or Hunter's, to put precisely.

"Any doubts?"

What a humble man to let his students ask him questions. And there went an entire army, including Scarlett and his admirers, circling his desk and buzzing like bees. On the other hand, someone was losing his ball on the sight.

We waited until everyone left.

"I don't think you waited for everyone to leave just to ask me questions. What can I help you boys with?"

His masculine voice would be wetting panties but not my cock. I felt sick to my throat, and my veins burned under my skin. Now that Hunter had run me down through his life, I had no respect for him.

Nile Clifford is the man who we psychos hate the most. These psychos are fuckers behind a mask, roaming with an elegant smile hiding a devil's mind. Fucking manipulators.

I hate liars the most. There is no fun in playing mind games and spending all the time on some worthless *one* when dominance can be exerted through sinister tricks, leaving a confused mind. Less hassle, high response.

"Are you aware of the ongoing murders of the Fifteenth that have been happening monthly for the last two years?" I was never a man to run around bushes. I know what I want, and if he doesn't speak, I have many ways to make him.

Nile smirked while putting the books and papers over the desk inside his leather briefcase.

"Boys, aren't you too young to be questioning me?" His smugness wasn't appreciated.

Hunter closed the door before marching to Nile's desk and holding him by the collar. I pulled my lighter out, playing with the spark wheel, the fire alarming out and extinguishing. The only way to keep me grounded other than my newfound addiction, *Lyric Kensely*, during the time my friend interrogates him.

"If there wasn't a camera, I'd hate to break your bubble that I am not the man you should be messing with, Hunter Owen. With great consideration, I am ordering you to remove your hands from me. NOW." There was authority, no doubt. The unfortunate fact, it wasn't going to shake me, or my pissed friend whose girlfriend admired someone other than him.

"SPEAK." I growled, done with the wordplay and power dance. No one is being seduced here with shit.

"I could easily have both of you killed and bankrupt in a single night. Play wisely boys, your angry hormones do nothing but make me laugh. Step back and act like mature men." These words can only be confirmed when a man asks the other to be mature. See their relationship status. The idea of defining maturity bespoke for those who hadn't had a taste of anarchy. Isn't he too old to not know, how addictive it is?

"Hunter, leave him, your rage will not make fuckers like him beg. Shit can walk the road naked but shameless like them would parade in pride. Let's talk in *his* terms of maturity... Fine with you, professor."

He gave me a once-over before nodding.

"Whatever fits you, Spade." His tone made me tilt my head and smile. Now, we are three mature men. Funny.

Hunter reluctantly left his collar, and he loosened his tie, breathing unevenly. Unlike Hunter, who had brutal muscles and was overbearing simply with a look at his presence, Nile was on the lean muscular side, one like my physique, but he was a taciturn man, which made him altogether a different side of nasty. In this spectrum of bad to worse, I am the middle ground.

"In my office."

We followed him to his office. Once inside, he locked the doors behind him and took his seat in front of us in his designated leather chair. We stalled sitting.

"You've got nothing to be wary of, sit down it'll take time." He grinned sinisterly, and against our conscience speaking to us, we took the guest seat across from him.

"I do not wish to repeat. Tell me, if you know anything about the murder of the fifteenth." I growled, losing my patience. I am supposed to be done with him soon and get to my father to open this mystery book in a better light. My girl needs me the most, and her among wolves is a darn threat making me mad.

One taste has chained me to her. I don't know what will

happen to me if anything happens to her.

"Surprisingly, Treyton Spade, I do know a lot about it. There is a catch, though," he licked his lips, grinning like a maniac high on vape.

"How long, nine months before you can let us on it?" I sneered.

He laughed, shaking his head in a motion of disbelief. "It'll be hard to piss me with words, Spade. I want you to know my information is expensive. I deal with a lot of sensitive information for many."

"Name your price." I wasn't lacking money, but what I lacked were some serious connections.

"Become an omen. You both, not just one. I presume this mafia lad has already let you in on my secret. Not everyone has the privilege to be a part of my hell, but I'm offering you a front seat. An invitation direct from the leader to enter the scythe insignia group." If he thought he was smart, I must say, he was. But I am not paddling my way into this mess of his.

"Thanks for your invitation professor, I'd like to decline as humbly as you offered." My whore gritted, and this conversation was going nowhere.

"Why is he acting like a wounded lion?" Nile sensed the thick hostility from my whore.

"You have his girlfriend in your class, and like any other she too, likes you. Professor Daddy." I sighed, noticing the impending headache. On the other hand, Nile laughed hard.

"Chill Lad, I'm not interested in little girls." This doesn't sound like a consolation to me.

"Yet, very much interested in girls." Hunter retorted.

"Right, and..." Nile smiled mischievously, however Hunter cut in between.

"She is, and that counts." Hunter glared, and Nile smirked. Their back and forth pushed my irritation to the surface.

"Why would you want youngsters like us?"

"Age is not my problem and your names are the reason. Infamous Owen crime family of London, and Spade family, a legacy of justice and law. No fool would let this combination walk away from their grasp." He made his point wisely.

"I don't want to." I rejected his offer completely.

"I could've helped, and your girlfriends could join as your

slave or Master or whatever your dynamic goes." His suggestions fell on deaf ears.

He whispered under his breath. Precisely, not happy with our response.

"Hunter Owen, you'll get my support. What else do you want? I'm not after your girl, and if you get to make her yours as an Omen, it means forever. You know the best." He came out successful because of something about Hunter that only he knew, and I wasn't aware of. Maybe it was a mafia power struggle, or maybe something else. I only know what Hunter lets me on.

"Fine, but I will not be following any of your society's stupid games."

"I don't like that. Let's do it this way, I'll give you both the information, and you guys prove to me you're capable of being a part. Accept the challenge." Nile was meticulous. Lover of his ways.

"And what that'd be?" I voiced, not liking how everything was being directed the way this man wanted.

"Kill the mastermind of the serial murder case, *Ghost Of Fifteenth*. That's your challenge, boys." Meaning, this game was instigated by a bloody elite in power.

"Name of the target." I clenched my jaw, trying to stop myself from reaching out to the lighter, warm in my pants pocket.

"Ramona Whistle." He pulled a cigarette out of his drawer and pressed the roll between his lips before looking at me.

"Do you think my lighter is to burn cigarettes?" This man annoys the hell out of me.

"If you're not using it to burn humans, at least use that fire to infect them." He motioned from his head, pointing to my pants, and I pulled it out, lighting it. The fire boomed in the air, high at a five-metre distance, and he whistled before letting his roll touch the surface and taking a long puff, he waited for my answer.

"You want to consolidate yourself in both the elite society of old money and the dark war of Mafia, the only reason you want us onboard with you." Hunter leaned back in his chair, tapping his fingers on the table.

Nile gave a glance at him and nodded, releasing the misty smoke from his puckered lips.

"You're known as *Supreme* in Omen." I waited for his

confirmation, and when he nodded again, the smile on my face creased in half-moon. "You're supreme, then make us Gods."

Hearing me, he choked hard, throwing his cigarette in the ashtray and drinking water. Hunter whistled in appreciation. The first time in our conversation, Nile finally lost his balls.

"You guys are a risky headache I am wilfully taking. That's so much I can do. Now you want to be Gods, why the fuck?" His bougie menace was torn from my one sentence.

"Supreme is the highest, above all. You nearly refer to yourself as the mighty entity who created everything, which practically you did. But you want the right power distribution because you've too many people of competence in your Hell, as you like to put it."

"And you wish to imply..." he was looking at me decisively. There was curiosity in his eyes, and I fed on that fire.

"Hunter and I bring that power on one table, giving you the balance. We deserve the title for that much work, *Professor*. Don't you think naming us Gods is the least you can do?"

He looked at me, smirked, and licked his lips. Smiling in a deep thought. Then he picked up his phone and sent a message to someone before focusing back on us. "You're a smart duo. Do you think, I am an idiot though?"

"Not that closely, Professor." I laughed.

"Bastards. I'll give you boys all the funds and time till you graduate. You'll receive the invitation to visit Omen on the ritual nights and once a month a task to achieve. Act as temporary members and after graduation join the society as a scythe insignia. Work for two years, and if you rise in status and power as a scythe member in the given time, I'll form the God division for you." He leaned back, crossing his legs and waiting for our response.

Fucker looks nice for once.

I shared a look with Hunter, and he blinked once, confirming the agreement.

"Done."

"Great to hear. One of my men will get in touch, and you'll receive an agreement attached to a procurement brochure. I've high hopes for both of you." He went silent, and we stood up, shook hands with him, and left the room.

The moment we stepped out, our phones buzzed with a message indication, and Hunter rolled his eyes.

"The bastard is cheeky." I chimed, parting from him and opening the message.

One agreement was confirming consent with detailed rules and another was an NDA.

The brochure I opened directed me to a link from where I switched tabs to a new one, and that was the site that had members' procurement, rules, and ritual night explanations. The site only opened through the one-time visit welcome link and showed the information after the one-time password was entered.

In no way would they take the risk of anyone being a legal witness or outing them. Second to that, none can take screenshots. Now, I get why this was a secret society.

OMEN

Insignia of death.

Membership Requirement

1. Memberships are only given through invitation.

2. Invitation to every new member is given with an assigned task to complete. Until then, the new member is under probation. In case of a task failure, details and procedures will be communicated.

3. The assignment to new members will include a game. The Player is allowed to use any method to prove their worth and must win the challenge.

4. The game involves the enactment of predator and Prey, i.e., a primal play game.

5. The Prey is the target of the assignment, and it must be dealt with before the set period of the task runs out.

6. Once the task's success is confirmed, a permanent membership, a group of operations based on the member's level, will be assigned.

7. The new members have to be present on their first ritual night, held once every month, to have their roles as either *Master or Slave* and *group insignia* assigned.

8. A new or permanent member cannot under any circumstances be allowed to skip the ritual night.

9. In unforeseeable circumstances, where the member cannot attend the ritual night, they must inform the concerned authorities prior to the ritual night scheduled for that month.

10. In case of a member willing to leave, Omen must meet the concerned authorities and provide compensation as per the final say of the concerned authorities.

Modus Operandi

1. The Supreme is the highest being, the creator of Omen. By every means, all the members are to submit and follow The Supreme.

2. The Supreme's words are the law of Omen.

3. The members of Omen work on assignments handed to them by *The Supreme*, who sanctions the requests from the authorities outside of Omen.

4. The members of Omen can give out special personal requests only through the screening done by the higher authorities and explicit permission from The Supreme.

5. Omen manages three levels of the ranking system to classify members into the same operating groups.

5.1. Scythe Insignia

5.2. Trident Insignia

5.3. Axe Insignia

6. Every member of the Omen must have the insignia allotted to them tattooed on their neck or their left wrist.

7. Only The Supreme has a reaper insignia tattooed on their place of choice.

8. The Master and Slave work in pairs.

9. The Master launders the money, transferring the assigned Prey's capital to the bank account provided by the officials of Omen. The Slave hides any proof and hunts the Prey if ordered by the Master or if the Master doesn't wish to accomplish the task themselves.

10. Master and Slave are in a submissive and dominant relationship where the Master is given carte blanche to manage their Slave.

Ranking System Rules

1. Scythe Insignia

1.1. The highest priority among the three insignia.

1.2. Follows a monogamous Master and Slave relationship.

1.3. Only deals with requests directly handed by The Supreme.

2. Trident Insignia

2.1. The second highest priority among the three insignia.

2.2. Follows the polygamous Master and Slave relationship.

2.3. Only deals with the request directly handed by the Omen officials.

3. Axe Insignia

3.1. Does not operate tasks on a priority basis.

3.2. Follows both polygamy and monogamy by the choice of Master and Slave in the relationship.

3.3. Only deals with requests made by overseas clients outside the Omen's chapter location.

Master And Slave Rules

1. The Supreme exists with no Slave.
2. Every Master and Slave are paired in an unbiased process through a randomised system.
3. A Master will be of higher status by power and economy in society than the Slave.
4. Masters must provide resources for the weekly/monthly tasks to their Slaves, and once every three months must execute one task by themselves.
5. A Master and Slave must wear a chain of branding given by each other, both on the premises of Omen and outside in public.
6. A Master and Slave will belong to the same insignia and, in specific and special cases, would have different insignia.

The Ritual Night Rules

1. The Master and Slave will be in a blood pact.
2. Once every month, the Slave on the ritual night will be hunted by the Master in a game of primal play, and after being hunted by the Master, the Slave must offer the libation of their

blood to the Master as a rule of blood pact.

3. Master must drink the blood of the Slave and fuck them on the altar on every ritual night, displaying exhibitionism in the rawest form as an enactment of predator and prey and claiming of territory.

4. The Ritual Night will be held once a month, and everyone will be given a letter signed by The Supreme a week before the scheduled night of rendezvous through an unmapped and unpredictable delivery.

5. If a member misses the ritual night on purpose, they will offer the Supreme their life through a game of hunt and chase led by the Supreme as the predator and the member as Prey. When caught, *The Supreme will take the member's life brutally, making an example out of them.*

6. On the ritual nights, the event will commence as mentioned below:

6.1. A task of the month and, in special cases, the task of the week will be assigned.

6.2. An auction for smuggled artefacts of the highest price on the black market will be held.

6.3. The next phase is the hunting grounds for the ceremony to begin with explicit permission from The Supreme.

7. On the night of the ritual, the Master will hunt the captured Prey of their task in the hunting ground and bathe the Slave in the Prey's blood to honour their blood pact and purify them before proceeding to clean them, dress them in expensive clothing and jewellery for the second phase of the ceremony.

8. Master will mix their blood in the water and drench the Slave's entire body from head to toe in the sacred concoction of their blood.

9. The hunting will proceed with rule 2, followed by rule 3, and then with a gallant meal together with The Supreme in the ballroom of Omen.

10. The Master and Slave may leave after the ritual, kissing The Supreme's hand as an act of making an oath of loyalty, respect, and devotion to The Supreme and Omen.

I sighed, sulking in the car seat. I don't know what to feel.

Joining a society didn't bother me, but the thought of Chipmunk dragged into the shenanigan makes me sick. Eventually, I have to talk to her and make it clear. She is my priority. An extension of myself, now that I have claimed her mine.

One hunt. Answers about the evil night of the fifteenth.

CHAPTER SIXTEEN

I wanted to have every possibility in my hands. The only that I did find was ceasing to exist.

"You're doing fine, Lyric. It's a process, and you've nearly completed it." She's a liar. Jessica diagnosed me wrong. All the truths were coming to light. Her lies were like satin, comforting but had a double side to it.

I forced a smile, sliding down in the therapy chair. I want to leave, and after what I heard earlier, what she plans to do tonight with Henry, I just want to be by Dad's side as soon as possible.

Unknown to her, I was standing by the gate when Henry was here. She thought just because it was her office, there would be privacy.

I remember every fucking word leaving her lips...

"Tonight, everything will be over, darling. I've tampered with Oberon's car. The moment he'd reach the highway, both his son and he'd die." He kissed her, their guttural moans filling in the room, turning my stomach. *How could he after what my father has done for him? He gave him a job and his brother a home to live in.*

Their voices still crawl my skin. Her moans when he fucked her on the very chair, I had to force myself to sit made my skin crawl. The invisible dirt of their body heat disgusts me. I don't want to contract any STIs because of them.

"Why're you staring at me?" Jessica licked her lips, tucking a stray brown lock behind her ear. She was like any ordinary girl who did her job and went home to rest before starting all over again the next day. Simple. Not. Who would think a nasty person homed in that body?

I slipped my purse on, reaching for the Ruby bracelet on my wrist to calm my anxiety. The idea of Treyton by my side assures me. He'd never know what I started feeling for him since the night he last visited me.

After talking to Ciro yesterday, I was positive. He said it was easy to find the truth, and it left me with a bright hope.

"This is your new medicine. I've changed the dose and informed your brother about it, too." Another lie. What I conclude, she must've increased the dose enough to kill me. Something tells me it has everything to do with the plan to assassinate my family.

In between the lines, I can read the simulation of their lie. *Lyric Kensely murdered her family under the influence of her madness.*

The image horrifies me.

"I understand. Thanks for always helping me." I smiled, and a discrete sense of humour played on my lips.

I stepped out of the room with another quick nod her way and rushed out of there down to the car waiting for me at the entrance.

"Where shall I take you next, miss?" The driver inquired politely but given what I'd heard, my suspicious eyes didn't leave him.

"Please take me to St. Evelyne University."

As he drove past different stops and turns, I pulled my phone out, sending a quick message to Ciro.

Lyric: *Meet me by the basketball court.*

Ciro was there, standing by the gates. As I got closer, the loud noises from inside the stadium indicated a game was going on.

"Ciro, it's urgent." I rasped, filling him in with everything I heard at the hospital.

A crease formed on his forehead, and when I finished narrating, his hands fisted.

"Anything else they were talking about? Some clue, why they're doing or on whose command?"

Those were the questions I needed an answer for. There was so much going on but the least I could comprehend, this plan was in the making for a long time.

"What did you gather?" My eyes were desperate at this moment. Some sort of consolation, but any would be enough.

"The case of the fifteenth is related to the fire incident twelve years ago. The people who died in the mansion where your father held his anniversary party, are the people you claimed to see, too. From what I gathered, they're not dead. There is a cult famous for doing illegal killings on contract. To make those deaths appear baseless without proper proof to carry on an investigation, they capture the injured victims by causing natural deaths. In your case, the fire was caused by the gas leak and cigarettes in the mansion, and during that hustle, they dragged the injured out of there. After treatment, they brainwash those people over the years and you know the rest, how those dead people become real-life serial killers."

It was my parents' last wedding anniversary—the final one before Dad was left to celebrate each year with nothing but a photo of Mum, a glass of wine, and lonely nights in his office. The last anniversary when I still had a family.

I reached for the bracelet, touching the jewel to calm my bubbling anxiety. My vision was closing up, and the surroundings blurred. I could hear Treyton's voice in my head and Ciro's voice in my ear. None helped, though.

"Treyton is aiming for the basket..."

The loud voices and cheers from inside were clear.

"Lyric, listen to me. I don't want you doing anything stupid. I promise I'll sort this out. Trust me." Ciro was close to begging but I don't know why. Ciro was never a person to soften his tone for anyone.

He was the crush I let go, the moment I knew about his undying love for his dead girlfriend. However, deep inside, he was hurting and the only person who understood my pain of losing someone. In this friendship, we shared everything or at least whatever was okay to tell the other.

Ignoring his calls, I walked inside the stadium and witnessed the crowd cheering for Treyton and his team. It was hard; there was no place to stand.

I slipped through the crowd and stood at the front, watching my man giving it his all, and dodging the players chasing after the ball in his hand.

My cheeks were moist seeing him. I don't know why I wanted to run and hug him tight. If this was Treyton withdrawal, I know why it was.

For a second, his eyes travelled to me, and our eyes locked.

His addictive whiskeys.

His addictive whiskeys watched me. I watched him too, and he turned, dribbling the ball, escaping the people and jumping high, scoring the ball in the net.

The crowd grew louder as their points raised.

Treyton's No. 4 jersey, I once dreamt of wearing to his game and proudly declaring to anyone who looked my way that he was mine. *My boyfriend.*

Dreams. Wishes.

It all has meaning until there is a possibility, and mine was non-existent.

"Lyric. You need to leave." Ciro's voice over the loud shouts brought me back to my senses. He grabbed my hand and pulled me out of the crowd.

I walked away, giving a glance at Treyton who was looking my way with a frown. I smiled through tears at him.

A fear was instilled: what if this was our last time?

I want to kiss him.

Something told me I'd regret not doing what I wanted. So, I snatched my wrist from Ciro's hold, turned to the crowd, and ran past people, ignoring the furious Ciro shouting behind me. He was following. I still ran and slipped past the guard towards the bench where the St. Evelyne team was resting before the last quarter.

"Treyton," I yelled his name, and the second he moved towards me, I jumped on him and planted my lips on his, taking him off guard.

He gradually moulded his lips to mine, indulging in the kiss. Devouring my mouth.

I kissed him with the same intensity. Tongues got involved, teeth nipped and sucked, our breaths ragged, and yet, we forbid to leave.

"Captain, we have to go prepare for next quarter. Make out with your girl later." He was one of the best players after Treyton.

On the other end, Ciro kept calling for me behind the guards, stopping his entry.

Reluctantly, I pulled apart from Treyton, and he gave me a quick kiss on my forehead. Whispering in my ear, "We'll talk as soon as I finish my game, Chipmunk. You are going to wait for me in your music room. Am I clear?"

He kissed me once again and glared at Ciro. His voice resonated in my ear, and I left with a heavy heart. However, I nodded, it stands true, he won't find me there.

"Do you have to leave, Dad?" I've been contemplating since afternoon how I'll explain it to Dad and Grayson to not leave.

There was no definite answer to this *how*.

"I'll be home soon, Lyric." My dad was back, the one who used to comfort my fears. The warmth of his hand on my head seeped into me, trying to fill the aching absence of love I had been yearning for.

"Worry not. The meeting is short, and he'll be home soon." Henry's guttural voice crawled under my skin, and I shuddered visibly.

"I don't want you to leave. Postpone it, please." I am falling behind on options to stop Dad, and Grayson is yet to arrive in the main hall. I hope that he senses the desperation in my voice and listens.

"This is important Lyric." Dad tried reasoning, but I won't be taking the short end of the stick. Not tonight.

"Everything is important, Dad. It always has been. You choose to prioritise everything over me. I am begging you for once, please don't go. Stay home. I need you." I cried and clutched his arm, denying to leave.

"What's all this ruckus, Lyric? You're not a baby anymore. Act mature." Grayson's voice boomed as he entered the hall.

Henry quickly did a curt nod to show respect, and I winced, still refusing to let go of Dad's hand.

"I don't care. I want you both home today, so stay." I shouted.

To my unfortunate luck, Grayson took a long stride my way and pulled me away from Dad. As my hold slipped, more furious tears stormed out of my eyes.

"Dad, don't entertain her antics. Jessica has already informed me, now that her doses are reduced, it may happen. If we indulge her, she'd act frantic and it won't be good." He seemed tired. The lines around his eyes exhibited exhaustion and frustration.

"No. It's not. I am not Gray, please... I beg you... Stay by my side. I need you, both. I beg you."

I witnessed my dad trying his hard to sustain his sanity through my cries, and Grayson fisted his hand to stop himself from touching me. I know how hard they were trying to control themselves.

"Let's leave, sir. We cannot afford to be late anymore." Henry pushed, glaring at me.

Dad came up to me and kissed my forehead. "I'll be home soon, baby."

"Let's have an *us* chat when I return." The us, in Grayson's words, returned after two years. A chat I was dying to have. He kept pushing me until today. What a nice time he chose that may be filled with regrets.

They were leaving me alone, again, to fend for myself.

Don't go. Don't leave me alone. Again.

I remember Ciro kept shouting through the ride home to not do anything stupid.

My phone blasted the entire afternoon with Treyton's

messages to wait for him tonight.

Majesty kept asking over the call why I sounded different just hours before Dad informed me he'd be leaving.

I decided what I had to do.

Running to the kitchen, I grabbed a knife and rushed to the awaiting car by the entrance of the mansion.

"Dad. Grayson." I yelled, focussing their attention on me.

I placed the sharp edge of the knife on my wrist.

They came to a standstill, their gaze locked onto me. For once, I was their priority.

"Lyric." Grayson, with a horrid expression, approached me.

Dad followed in his footsteps. Equally struck by what I was trying to attempt.

"Baby, let go of that knife." Dad pleaded, his voice breaking.

I shook my head, refusing to withdraw. Crying, to be his priority.

"Don't go." I was shaking, digging the edge on my wrist, and a piercing cry left my lips in pain. *Red dropped.*

"Lyric, let go. Please, don't hurt yourself."

Red poured.

"Baby, fine. We won't."

Red burned.

"Sir, Jessica said you cannot indulge her."

"Fucking shut up Henry. That's my sister."

Impatient voices. Accusing. Cursing. Panicking.

Dad, Grayson, and Henry's voice meddling in, I knew I needed more than a wrist slit to become a priority.

Placing the knife on my throat, I slit myself.

It scared me until...

Red became me.

I became red.

"Lyric!!!"

I am their priority.

CHAPTER SEVENTEEN

"Protect her, Treyton. She is vulnerable, and their easy target." Sullen words of my father stabbed my chest.

My mother, who hated Lyric moments before, composed her shaken stance upon hearing what occurred on the fifteenth of the last month.

"It has to be a joke. That girl is being targeted and enduring the blasphemy alone." She gazed at me strangely.

My father filled me in on how the serial murder case of the fifteenth is related to an arson twelve years back, the cult whose leader's name Nile gave me. The broken pieces finally fell together, making the big picture.

I've been pondering all day after Lyric left me with her disobedience. She didn't wait.

Yanked out of my train of thought, I shot a look at my dad. Out of nowhere, my phone on Dad's home office table chimed with Hunter's call. Seriously, could the timing be any worse?

I ignored, getting back to the conversation with my father

when his call again flashed on my phone screen.

"You should pick up." Mom suggested, reading my irritation.

I did, holding the phone against my ear. "What do you need?"

"Lyric attempted suicide." His words were emotionless. Nothing about it was different, and still held the power to annihilate me.

"This. Isn't. A. Joke." I rasped, angry veins popping on my neck.

"And it's not. She is in the hospital and I've texted you the location. Hurry. Her condition is critical." There was pain in the cold voice, one he never easily let loose.

I was still reeling from the news. She attempted suicide.

Her kiss.

She was crying.

Her fears.

The haunted gaze in her lonely orbs.

I wanted to ask *why*.

The monster in me wanted to beg her, too, and ask what was hurting her?

I'd burn the world for you, were the words I desperately wished to tell her.

She is my priority. Then why couldn't she tell me?

"Treyton... Baby, are you crying?" Mom's panic shook me.

"Treyton... Champ, are you okay?" Dad's surprise made me realise the tears that, for once, made me feel more human than a monster wrapped in flesh.

"I am not. Lyric attempted suicide." My chest ached. My breath was barely there, suffocating me. "Take me to her," I begged. I needed to know.

I tried regulating my breath through the haze until I reached the hospital. A corpse operated in my stead.

There in front of me was Grayson and her dad, Oberon.

I ran to them, pinning Grayson by his collar on the nearest wall. His red shirt was the living proof she suffered. How scared she must've been.

"Why did this happen? What did you do to her?" I roared, punching him in the face, shoving any hand that tried to restrict my movements. I punched. Punched. Punched and punched his face blue and purple. He didn't retaliate. How could he... *the bastard failed her.*

"Treyton, enough. You should focus on why you're here." Dad chided, pushing me away from him, but the red I saw turned volatile.

Henry. He watched from the corner, terrified. I shoved Dad's hand and marched to him, punching his face repeatedly. Unlike Grayson, his expressions were pained. I beat the shit out of him till he was unconscious.

They hurt her.

They caused pain to my Lyric.

They'll pay for the red she painted with her fear and ache. With her tears and loneliness.

"Treyton Spade. Enough!!! The more you try doing anything, the more likely you are to cause harm to her." Dad yelled, ripping me away from murdering Henry.

I wasn't in my right mind. I don't want to hear them. The more they speak, the more it aches my chest.

I burst out of that nightmare, abandoning the bloody wreckage that failed to deliver any semblance of justice for my girl!

The sole entities that thrust in my veins were her tears and the picture of red painted through Grayson's shirt.

Please, live Lyric. Your God commands you to live, and your God promises you your vengeance will be his.

Tonight, the colour of revenge will be fiercer than the red she poured in agony.

Judgement shall be made.

They've angered Lyric Kensely's God. Their sin will stay forever. It'll burn with them.

"I knew you'd come. Everything is prepared."

When I entered the extravagant building, the reality simmered. The smell of revenge wafted fresh in the air.

Hunter's men walked me to the deepest, hidden part of the mansion he operated from.

A dungeon.

A dark lair of the bad guys of the mafia world, among which

their lord was seated on his throne over a chair in a cosy home office theme with shelves and a fireplace. Nothing about the setting spoke gore other than the floor that was painted red.

"I caught him yesterday. You were right about his new cartel. It became easy to sabotage little filthy lizards. He and Henry operated together." He was listing his sin, and I pulled my lighter out of my pants pocket.Letting the flame loose as it burned furiously. Nothing will be stopping this one.

"Henry and Romano are brothers. Their well-wisher's wife became their enemy and died during delivery surprisingly, when she got a hold of their nasty deeds and how they were trying to ruin the Kensley name and attempting to transfer their wealth in the accounts of dead men in their captivity."

That wasn't astonishing anymore.

"Since dead tell no tales, tracking becomes as difficult. They've been using this underhanded trick for a long time in different countries until they stumbled upon Kensely's domain. It would've been easy if Grayson wasn't so strict about his father's work and procedures and sanctioned everything in the name of helping his father. These guys have been honing the plan since the day they met them twelve years ago and it all started with a fire in the mansion." Hunter went on, providing me with the intricate details about tonight's plan and how they were ready to make Lyric their scapegoat. They medicate her to brainwash and play with her mind every fifteenth until she becomes mad in reality.

They abducted her from the safety of her own home, cleverly staging a scene that forced her to bear witness, pushing her to the brink of insanity while syphoning off her wealth. For far too long, they've been poisoning her, hollowing her out piece by piece.

It would've been perfect if not for Lyric Kensely attempting suicide. Perfect if she didn't stab my father. Perfect if she didn't meet me.

Everything happened. It happened for a reason. And I was meant to believe the lies of the girl who wasn't a liar.

"I must clap. What a master plan that requires both patience and time. I wouldn't have been able to do this. You brothers nailed it. Immaculate." I clapped, gritting my teeth and kicking him in his gut.

He was drenched in his blood. His wounds made him unrecognisable.

"Now, hear me. I'll kill you. Give death to an undeserving like you, and your brother will go behind bars. Your so-called cult created to kill on contract is already on its way to demise. My father has the paperwork ready to make it happen. The next phase of the story is exciting..." I clicked my tongue, kicking him in the face. The lighter burned in my hand, itching me to put him on fire.

"I've wired the remaining proof to your dad, how some cult members were officers and helped escape the hiding killer in the house. We still don't know the reason of writing over the wall and choosing the particular place, but you take your time, the second she wakes up, Scarlett will inform us."

How Scarlett never came to know about him and his dark side was still a surprise to me. Not the thought I'd entertain.

"Where was I... Uh-huh... The next phase... Your brother and his whore in the prison dead. How?"

"A fire accident happened. Leaked gas and short circuit." Hunter completed me, smirking.

"And being burned alive is said to be one of the most painful pain. But it wouldn't be as painful as what my girl had to endure tonight. Your pain would never be able to compensate for hers."

I don't want this man's blood on my hand. Beating him into a pulp was rightfully done by Hunter. I was here to finish off what he started. Pain play.

I stepped away as the men in black started pouring burning oil on his languid body. His screams turned into wheezing. Not enough pain.

"Tell your God, you were punished by her God. He'd understand." I tossed the lighter on him, and flames lapped high in the air with the strong stench of burning flesh.

"May the sinner never find peace. Amen." Hunter made a cross sign and murmured a prayer under his breath.

Hours passed, and I watched the body turn into ashes. The flesh turned to a mass of nothingness. Black ashes like his heart that corrupted my girl's world.

Now, her pain comes to an end.

"It's over."

It did.

Within an hour of receiving every proof, Henry and Jessica were arrested. Dad promised he'd bring justice to my Chipmunk, and he made sure to keep it.

But there was no guarantee about how Lyric was doing. The moment I turned the T.V. off, Hunter put me on a conference call with Scarlett in the hospital. The news was a mess from the chaos surrounding the murder of the fifteenth and Lyric's tragic suicide. Yet, we still dared to wish for a miracle, somehow for her to be rescued from this nightmare. For her to be saved.

I couldn't wait outside those doors. It was a pain greater than I ever imagined. A pain that was much more intense than I felt sitting outside during my father's surgery.

I'd faint if I was there. I knew.

I loved her more than words could justify and emotions could prove.

"Scarlett. How is she?"

Was it vulnerability in my voice?

"She is doing better. Fortunately, Grayson stepped in just in time, as the doctor said, and she missed a vital artery. They'll keep her under observation. You can visit her tomorrow."

My knees gave up. I slumped on the ground in a distorted heap of uncontrollable emotions.

"You should be thanking God." Hunter made me laugh at his sarcasm.

"I need your help." My abruptness turned his frown quizzical.

"With?"

"Kidnapping."

CHAPTER EIGHTEEN

Three words.

He. Kidnapped. Me.

I was supposed to be discharged and back home with my family.

Dad and Grayson's reaction when I woke up was insane. They kept on apologising and asked for my forgiveness. Piece of news: I never hated them. They are my family, the only people left by my mom to me.

I know why they acted so... Jessica was the reason. She instructed them.

Just like you shouldn't indulge schizophrenia, she sweet-talked them into believing her therapeutic approach.

She's in her deserving place now, rightfully, behind bars together with Henry.

If my suicide was the only way to get back my life, I would've done it before. Let's say using some blood bag or ketchup instead of bleeding myself. At least pre-planned, and I would've a guaranteed survival chances. Not like this one. This time, I barely showed the middle finger to the reaper, and he might be pissed.

"I'm home, Chipmunk."

Anywhere but here, in Treyton's presence. Can you believe that lowlife? The scoundrel didn't bother to show his face even once during my entire hospital stay!

I kept looking at the door of my ward in the hope he'd come. Not when his parents stopped by, too, and his mother apologised for her behaviour towards me.

Her dilemma was understandable, if it was Treyton and I, the reaction would've been the same. And my prediction was correct. Lavender is a warm person. We met under ridiculous circumstances.

"What did you do today, Chipmunk?" His seductive smile and addictive eyes are a lethal mixture. His face, the cherry on a chocolate fudge cake. His voice is out of a sexy audiobook, and he is the very definition of a perfect piano piece.

Factually, he has no problem. Physically, he causes others a problem, but my friend mentally... Mentally, he is the problem.

"This and that," I shrugged, strumming a new tune to fit the music I plan to release this autumn.

Who'd think this guy owned a penthouse, bought a vintage piano, carved my name and my mother's favourite flower on it, and designed a music room *for me*?

The piano was crafted from the same type of wood as my mother's piano. He expressed his regret for his actions, a sentiment I never expected to hear.

Also, he has a private basketball on the rooftop where I can get front-row seats and an HD view of his beautifully half-naked and shirtless body when he practises.

Couple goals?

We're not. He never mentioned anything. Pretended kidnapping and locking me in the high tower of Rapunzel was *normal*.

"And..." He trailed, resting his head in my lap, sitting on the floor while I played another minor note.

"And...?" I smirked, portraying my innocent face and confusion at best.

"And what else, Chipmunk?" He played with the basketball ball in his hand, rolling it on the floor, waiting patiently.

If he thinks playing house and being timid is my thing, he got the wrong person.

"Does sending your dad your nudes, count?" My smile crept wide, and I played a dramatic note.

I watched him from my peripheral. He closed his eyes, gritting his teeth, and jolted straight up, facing me.

"Chipmunk!!!" One could taste his wrath in the air.

I licked my lips mischievously and stood up to leave the room. That's how I ended our conversation the past four days.

I leave the room.

"You mailed Hunter sex position books in my name. Emailed Grayson your drowning voicemail. You made my mother believe I ran over someone with my bike and got arrested, and had Ciro file my missing report. Is this what you address as mature?" The more his overpowering self evaded my stance, the more I acknowledged how close he was. I'm within his hands' reach.

He refused to touch me, though. He has not touched me in a way I know he does. Neither his addictive whiskeys tamed my unnerving heart.

"I found you. How much will I get?" A cunning smile embraced my lips.

"Chipmunk, I am serious." He gave me his typical death glare, even though he knows it doesn't work on me. Fun fact: I don't even have to see his face anymore to know exactly what expression he's making. His voice leaves no room for imagination—I can tell just from the different tones and pitches when he talks.

I halted mid-way, turning to stand toe-to-toe with him. Meeting his eyes. Drinking his hard expression.

"We talk Treyton. However messed up it gets, we always talk. Communication is our thing Treyton Spade and you're jeopardising it. If we cannot, we give space. But neither of us beat around the bush. That's not the kind of person you're or I am." I poked my index in his chest, furious.

He has trapped me in this house where I have access to every luxury but no access to the outside world. A cocoon I never chose.

Guards stop me whenever I try to leave, and among them, the female guards are not very friendly. They are kind enough to be wary of my barely there healing injury, and I possibly celebrate at that.

"Then what am I supposed to do? What would make you stay by my side? How will I know you're not going to do anything stupid again? Why are we again at the round of questions and you dodging each one of them?"

I paused. His eyes glistened under the setting sunlight. I antagonised him for not knowing. For making me wait.

What if I had waited for him that day?

What would've changed?

The haze of red submerging him was different than mine. It was burning in his fire. And I reeled in the foci of what elapsed.

The question that was mocking me, and I hated to admit it.

How I was proven innocent?

How did Henry and Jessica's deed come to light?

Who killed the cult leader reported in police statements?

Why Jessica and Henry were caught in a fire accident in prison?

How the agonising pain of the past two years of my life ended in one night?

"Lyric." He cupped my face gently, rocking in his embrace and I was melting.

"Treyton," I cooed, reaching to the parts of his inner beast that speak to me. Only me.

Addictive whiskeys hunted my chestnuts in an unbreakable trance. I don't want to break free from this man who brought me heaven when all I knew was hell.

"You became my extension, and I don't know how to cut you out without killing myself. I exist with you and cease to be without you. I know love because it's your face that makes it possible to visualise. You ruined me, Lyric Kensely. You brought this God on his knees for you. I asked you to live because, without you, I don't know how to. You're my priority. You're my reason."

I was stunned. My eyes that occasionally are emotional found a new reason to cry.

Love has never wrapped its arms around me so fiercely! When I was lost and alone, he found me, claiming me as his own and turning me into his everything, filling my life with warmth I never knew existed.

Why did he believe a liar?

"I love you, too. I don't have impressive words encrusted like you, so manage with what I have." I kissed him deep and intense.

Our lips moulded. Bodies collided. He held me down, laying me on the floor.

It was hurried. Messy. Starved.

Clothes ripped. Bodies tangled. Moans filled the entirety of the common hall. He thrusts, and I took him all. It was raw, rough, and anything like he treated me the first time.

I savoured him like his good girl.

"I saw red." He explained how that very night rolled out with every detailed sentence, while thrusting inside me like a wild beast.

He hurts for me.

"I will burn this world if something ever happened to you." He groped my breasts and tortured me under the wet touch of his mouth, sucking them and his hand playing me like his personal slut.

He smiles for me.

"The thought of losing you scares me." He rotated his hips, tenaciously stimulating all my sweet spots, and I screamed, drawing closer to the higher.

He pulled out and went between my legs, showing the magic of his lips on my clit and weeping hole he just fucked into ecstasy. My hands on his locks instigated him to do his worst.

He taught me how painfully pleasurable it could get if he owns my pleasure and pain.

"You're the one I want to see when I wake up and go to sleep. It doesn't come with a negotiation. This is how we are going to be."

He sees me when I fade into the crowd.

I climaxed several times, but it was barely enough. He flipped me on my stomach, and his bite marks ached on my skin. My nipples rubbed against the cold floor, eliciting a loud moan.

I watched him walking to our bedroom to return with his favourite lighter and wax stick, which I have a hazy memory of.

The hunger was flowing both ways.

He needed me.

I needed him.

To me, love has become Treyton. And Treyton has become love.

I don't know if he's a bad guy or the hot God.

He is Treyton Spade. My filthy confession of love. My man and that's all that matters.

"Ahhh... Fuck... God, yes..." I screamed, and he slapped my arse, going down between my legs. His one hand pressed on my nape, and the other jabbed three fingers inside my mouth. He thrusts his fingers, reaching to the back of my throat.

Gradually, leaving my nape, he spanked me repeatedly until I was a moaning mess of tears and saliva dripping from my lips.

Despite my desperate attempt to run from his hold, he kept me pinned to the floor. His knees pressed down on my thighs, keeping me unmoving.

"You cannot escape your God, Chipmunk." He laughed in that unhinged voice, and a visible shiver tickled my spine.

A muffled, painful moan wheezed out of my lips. He was still jamming my mouth with his fingers, and I could feel the hot burning wax on my arse cheeks and thighs.

It was scorching, and yet my pussy wept shamelessly to be touched by him.

Another melted drop froze on my skin, and I cried in pain that followed the pleasure. Shifting me at an angle where his knee rubbed my pussy from behind, the repeated narration of erotic screams and moans of pain and pleasure mixed with filthy laughter and grunts of Treyton excited both of us.

I am not a girl of kink. With him, though, meaning and definition changes. They find their possibilities to exist. Countless possibilites.

"You like it, right, Chipmunk?" He rasped in my ears, panting.

With a gentle nod of confirmation from me, his smile painted behind my closed lids.

"Such a good fucking slut." He licked my ear and slipped his fingers out of my mouth.

I blinked, observing his skin bleeding around his fingers from my teeth mark. He didn't care about them and pressed the wet fingers from my saliva in between the crack of my arse cheeks.

"Someday, I'll fuck this virgin hole, too." He growled and, holding me up by my waist, pressed my back against his front. Both of us were on our knees as he thrust inside my wet, swollen pussy. His dick going deeper than before.

I panted, trembling in his hold. Feeling every inch of him squeezed inside of me.

He licked the column of my neck and sucked on the crook where my shoulder and neck meet. His other hand pinching my nipples and fondling my breasts.

I was ravished completely, collapsing when he came into the nth condom. Only he could stash a box in every corner, and the idea fucks me up because I could already picture myself on every surface of this house, spent and sore, similar to what I was enjoying now. The after tremors and care.

He brought us to our room we came to share. The master bedroom.

Sitting in the bathtub together, dipped in warm water filled with sea salt and coffee essence, Treyton massaged my shoulder, and I was moaning whenever he touched any hickey.

"I was meaning to ask, so you're a member of a secret society?" My eyes were closed, and my head rested on his chest.

"Not yet, but yes. I am. Does that make you feel different?"

To him, my opinion matters the most.

"No. You chose to save me, Treyton. Never caring how the aftermath of your actions would unfold. So, I have decided to follow the path with you. Secret society thing thrills me, and I know you'll never let harm come my way." I kissed his chest, loving the feel of his hands on my skin and how his heart beats in synchronisation with mine.

"Your imagination," he laughed, caressing my waist, adding to his statement. "I'd never let anything happen to you, Chipmunk. You're my equal." He kissed my forehead. The only confirmation I'd ever need.

"I trust you."

We kissed again in the bathtub and fucked again in the shower.

With Treyton, life wouldn't be normal. And I was looking forward to my not-so-boring life.

CHAPTER NINETEEN

"Is this alright? Should I change?" My nerves were playing a rhythm off-beat, and I was no better with my anxiety piling up.

Treyton creased out his suit and addressed me.

"You look gorgeous, Chipmunk. There's no need to change." He kissed my shoulder, running his fingers through my open locks, and I melted in the monotonous rhythm. He has a way with his touch; it works on me like magic.

I gave myself a last look in the mirror. The elegant red dress paired with black heels reminded me of the first time I tried it in the store.

Treyton was impressed that I dressed in everything he adorned me with, from the ruby jewellery to the heels and dress. Not to forget, my new black nails were quite the statement. Lavender went as far as arguing with her son right there in the salon, just to claim her right to pick my nail style.

"Chipmunk, let's leave." He shouted from downstairs, and I rushed, taking only the invitation with me.

Tonight, phones or anything that doesn't belong to Omen or would connect us to the outside world were prohibited. My nerves rattled from thinking about what would unfold on the Omen grounds, and my only anchor was my boyfriend.

"Deep breaths, Chipmunk. Take a quick nap, and I'll wake you up when we're there." He tried his best. Plus one for the endeavour and minus hundred for the advice.

Despite my mind rejecting the action, I closed my eyes. The sweet smell of Treyton's cologne and his continuous caress on my thigh lulled me into a dreamless sleep.

Thwack.

I could hear voices. Violent voices.

Forcing my eyes open, I looked around. The room was pitch black, entirely covered in the night of sin.

Slap.

In front, there was a stage and beautiful artefacts appeared. The loud noises around me finally registered.

An auction was taking place, and the people around were bidding. Piece by piece, the ornaments I never have seen anything like queued on stage, and irrespective of how high the price was, crazy bidders were running after them.

I gulped, silently watching the mind game of money, drawing in hungry wolves. Their aura was intimidating; taking it in was enough to shake me. Neither of them looked like someone you'd dare laugh at. People of power from every field possible on earth were sitting there.

"Hope you had a great time, Masters and Slaves. Now please, move to the ceremonial ground, for the ritual night."

Everyone stood up and started walking out from the door as the curtains pulled, illuminating the dark room from the infiltrating lights.

My senses jammed to conclude anything logical after what I witnessed, and I searched for the man I came with. I looked around in the bare minimum light, trying to figure out who my boyfriend was in the crowd.

By the time everyone left, the room was empty, and no one was there other than the staff. My jittery nerves clawed on my skin. Sweat slipped from the corner of my forehead.

"Excuse me..." I flinched to see a man in a butler uniform. He looked at me with a vicious gaze and, sporting an emotionless face, continued. "Please join the members on the ceremonial ground."

"Do you know where the man I came with went?"

He pulled out a tab from his side, asking me for the name. I did and waited, but to my dismay, he stated there was no one registered with the specified name and, if I was sure, there was a man with me.

The knowledge of being alone in this dangerous place and having Treyton not by my side fucked my logical self. I couldn't configure my next move. I was clueless.

"Hurry to the ground." He replaced his robotic tone with an assertive one, and I was forced to oblige.

I walked to the outside of the mansion, following the route made between the thick and lush trees on either side. The marble stones placed in a pattern led me to the crowd of people standing in pairs in the middle. They all faced the beautifully arranged stone altars. Opposite the altars—each engraved in a different language—stood a gothic mansion in the distance.

My breath choked between admiring the architecture and the situation I was trapped in and drifted to the second-floor balcony, large enough to accommodate half this crowd. The doors to the very place opened, and maidens dressed in the maid costume and men in a butler suit lined up.

A man created to rival Adonis stepped in front, close to the balustrade, looking down on the crowd as if he was the king and we were the peasants of his creation.

Have I seen him?

The idea popped and disappeared soon when my eyes drifted behind him, spotting Treyton and Hunter. They appeared bigger than the sun itself. Unapproachable. Majestic but in the most wrong way. They were there but barely in human clothing. What lurked in their darkness were trapped monsters begging to be freed.

My eyes met with addictive whiskeys, and I felt lost. He was distant, unlike my boyfriend, whose eyes reflected my image. *Who was he?*

"Lyric!!" I looked at Scarlett, magically appearing from somewhere, and standing just as confused as I was. "What's Hunter doing up there? He left me alone in the auction hall. That bastard," she groused, glaring behind me at the balcony.

I couldn't make myself look at Treyton again. The look in his eyes haunted me.

"We will commence with the ritual. The slaves must wait in the compound grounds for their masters naked to purify them." The voice booming from the man in authority shook me.

Breathing, I faced the balcony again. I dreaded what I'd witnessed on Treyton's face, but he wasn't there anymore. Neither Hunter nor Scarlett, who disappeared from beside me.

Fear started its play when slaves stripped down to nothing and went on their knees. Masters left the ground.

I was the only one standing. Spotting Scarlett in the extreme corner, stripped naked and on her knees.

I felt a shiver run through me as I sniffled, struggling to keep my voice from cracking. I yanked my dress down, fumbling as I took off my lingerie and heels. What was I even doing?

A maid came to me, and I handed my belongings and jewellery reluctantly. The only essence of calm I had.

Sitting on my knees, I waited, shaking under the cold breeze of the night.

Thump.

Clicks.

Thwack.

Loud sounds closed on the compound ground, and I hugged my naked body, shaking like an autumn leaf.

Where is Treyton?

I promised him I'm together in this, and yet, as the moon shifts, something dies in me. I just want to see him, that's all.

Panicking, I couldn't properly make out the shoes that stopped in front of me and looked up.

“Treyton,” I wheezed. He was holding a chalice in his hand, and in that second, he was the God. My God.

"Eyes close, Chipmunk." The command, followed by the endearment, consoled the scared part of me.

I obliged, closing my eyes, and the thick liquid of oxidised iron resembling blood poured from my head down my body, slipping between my breasts and pooling on my thighs, drained from the crack of my legs.

My breath shuddered, and I slowly opened it to see my hands and legs red. My breasts and hair dipped in the thick rustic liquid. The horror of it being human blood registered, and not some chemical.

I gasped, facing Treyton, who picked me up bridal style and carried me to the fountain placed in the corner.

I watched silently. Convincing myself to observe.

Masters soon enough gathered in the compound, pouring the chalice filled with blood on their slaves. I shook my head, deviating my eyes from the monstrous ceremony to Treyton. He placed me under the running fountain water, and the fresh blood that nearly nauseated me mixed with the water and washed off my body.

"Treyton..."

He shook his head, signalling me not to speak. "Not now, Chipmunk."

I knew better than to go against his words. He escorted me inside the gothic mansion and to one of the rooms where my belongings were already kept.

Instead of stopping, he walked me inside the bathroom and settled me in the bathtub.

"Wash yourself." He directed calmly, observing as I washed myself carefully and changed into my clothes.

Later, he offered his hand, and entwining my fingers with his, I stalked his every step. He brought us to the compound, and I tightened my grip on him. Scared to let go.

Quickly, Treyton kissed my shoulder, comforting me from his touch.

The butlers and maids then brought a bowl filled with water and a dagger in a gold-plated tray. I had no idea when Treyton slit his hand from the dagger and poured his blood into the water. Memories fresh from the night when he claimed me his flashed in front of my eyes.

The transparent liquid turned blood red. Treyton picked up the bowl and poured it all over me. I gasped, shivering under the cold water trickling down my body. Breathing through the process, my eyes were fixed on him.

The addictive colours of whiskey watched me, and a sly grin played secretively on his lips. It suggested, *this is an us thing.* I wanted to laugh but remained mute.

Once done, he stepped back and leaned his face close to mine.

"Run. Chipmunk."

I had already played this a thousand times in my head since the day Treyton told me about primal play. Both thrilling and corrupting me in the delicious darkness.

I took off, rushing past him without looking back, and disappeared into the woods. The eerie woods were filled with screams, splashes of blood, and moans.

My chest burned when I thought to have covered a mile, my feet throbbing from running so fast in heels.

I halted and snuck in between the two bushes behind a large tree, looking as a Master chased his Slave and grabbed her by the hair, pushing her into the dirt on the ground. She screamed, trying to hit him and run, but to no avail. He overpowered her.

I placed my hand on my mouth, muffling any voice that bubbled in my throat, witnessing cruel sex, where he ripped her dress and fucked her as if she was a toy and not a human being screaming. Whenever she complained it hurt, he'd hit her head on the ground.

I don't know if it was consensual or not, but honestly, with everything going on and where we were, I couldn't have cared less. After all, what do I know about this world I stepped into other than believing in my boyfriend and his sacrifice?

"Chipmunk, too bad." The creepy voice embraced me from behind, and I sprinted forward in the hope of losing him again.

I could hear Treyton laughing when I ran. He was close, so close, it nearly scared the shit out of me.

I turned around the two crooked trees and crossed two Masters who had one Slave, both fucking her from front and behind. The picture of polygamy revolted me, but to each their own, who was I to question?

"Arghhh..." I screamed when a powerful hand whisked me by my arm and pushed me to the ground.

I know the rule: slaves aren't to be touched other than their masters, and the relief melted my bones.

"I caught you, and now, I'll fuck you." He growled and grabbed me by my hair, ripping my dress, and dragged me through the mud to the stone altar.

I never knew this would entail, when I thrashed and pushed Treyton's touch, he'd still go for it. It was as if my mind denied and sipped on the adrenaline rush, but my body was ready to be fucked and owned by him. This was the trust of ours that whatever happens, we're safe in each other's hands.

He laid me on the stone, grabbed his favourite lighter from the pants pocket, and burned my tattered dress and lingerie to ashes. I laid naked in heels and jewellery like a trophy.

Licking his lips, he hovered over my body and bit hard on my lower lip. My blood seeped into his mouth, and he suckled like a vampire baby.

My fingers tore through his shirt impatiently, shredding the fabric, and we became needy and desperate for each other.

Pushing him, I sat up, straddling him and kissing as intensely as he reciprocated. A hungry battle of tongue and naked bodies tangled. Water dripping from my hair dropped on him.

"Fuck, my sexy slut." He groped my breasts, fondling them. With his every touch, I forgot that there were people around, each equally naked and watching us. To me, only he and I existed.

He sucked on my nipple, and I moaned loud. Many who didn't seem in the mood much started fucking their slaves hearing me. Ignoring all of them, I felt this powerful being who had all the authority tonight, and it was him who surrendered to me. My God was on my mercy.

"Spread for me, and take my cock like a good girl. Every second I fuck you, address me as your God, and thank me. Show me your gratitude." The octave in his voice dropped to a deadly chill.

I panted when Treyton thrusted inside me. His body heat seeped within mine, and his dick stretched me deliciously.

"Oh, God. Thank you." I cried loudly, and wrapping my hair around his wrist, he laid me back on the stone and inched further inside, hitting the sweet spots.

The loud sound of squelching, his balls slapping against my arse every time he pushed deeper lined tears of ecstasy in my eyes.

Sinking my nails deep in his back, I enjoyed his groans and wrapped my legs around his hip. He fucked me into oblivion and pulled out, drenching me in his cum.

I smiled, breathless, and he smirked, licking his lips.

"Another round."

Thank you, my God.

CHAPTER TWENTY

The delicious smell wafting from the kitchen and my man shirtless dicing vegetables for soup and salad was appetising. My stomach grumbled for food, and my pussy throbbed from the view.

"Trying to impress my dad with your cooking, boyfriend." I licked my lips, leaning on the fridge behind me and checking Treyton out.

It's been a year since Treyton, and I moved in together. When I told my father about us and my decision to live with Treyton, he wasn't very happy nor to know his daughter's boyfriend kidnapped her after her healthy discharge from the hospital.

Grayson didn't say much and talked to Treyton alone in his room, a *man-to-man conversation*.

Either way, he was able to convince our father that it was time I started living like an adult, and if ever need be, my family would be there waiting at the same place for me. And something great did happen out of it. I get to have a father-daughter date twice a week. A promise he made a long time ago and was finally keeping it.

"I can try not to." He smiled, stirring the pot on the stove. I guess that's lamb stew.

"You need brownie points though," I walked closer and hugged him from behind, nuzzling my face in his back.

"What else could he give me when I have you, Chipmunk?" Treyton Spade is fluent in flirting. None would perceive him as a cheesy talker. However, he is and does the cheesiest things.

Last year, on my birthday, he gave me twenty-one letters and twenty-one gifts and ended the night with a romantic dinner. Each of his letters had something he loved about me and the last letter was a special message. *Thanks for taking birth. You're the perfect birthday gift I'd been looking for myself.*

I've kept all those letters and presents stored in my music room. They're special. However, this year, I plan to make his birthday unforgettable, too, because his special day was the day after I attempted suicide. In the chaos, he didn't remember and had a simple meal with his parents, where he took ownership of his house and financial assets.

"Smooth talker," I grumbled, enjoying his body heat.

"Dishes are done. We've to arrange the dinner table before everyone arrives." He turned around, facing me, and kissed my forehead.

I was still in my pyjama shorts, tired from yesterday's party held for Dad's second time becoming Mayor. Who'd believe, at the end of the Day, Treyton proposed to have a family meal with him and me at our place.

I spent the entire day cleaning the house despite my boyfriend repeatedly pleading we can hire a housekeeper. Albeit, I hate the idea. If he said it's a family gathering, I don't want anything to be done by someone else, and the pretty decorations I did when Treyton was busy cooking is one of them.

"Let's wash up. I need to fill myself with your anarchy so, the entire night my body wouldn't itch to hold you close, trap you in our room, and fuck your moans for everyone to hear." His filthy mouth worked on the column of my neck, and I was more than ready to be eaten.

"Someone is early for dinner," I chuckled, tracing his cock over his shorts that painfully grew beneath my touch.

"Fuck. Yes, Chipmunk." He groaned, sliding his hands down my waist to my arse, groping the cheeks, and pulling me towards him.

His dick rubbed against my stomach, and I moaned. My pussy convulsing, eager to be touched.

"Jump."

I followed his command, and he caught me mid-air, wrapping my legs around his waist.

"Pull my cock out, and stroke."

Another command I gladly followed. He walked us upstairs to the second floor of the penthouse, where our room was. I stroked him, smearing the gathered precum on the tip of his veiny and bulbous dick all over the angry purple length that abuses me on every surface with the most delicious strokes.

He pressed his lips harder on my neck, biting and licking the area. Another hickey my father wouldn't be happy to see. He already assumes Treyton is a sex addict. Only my brother accepts that, genuinely, Treyton is Lyric addict.

Grayson has started trusting him; I don't know since when. The fact I am aware of, and he pointed, "Lyric, he is the only man, in whose eyes, I see my sister the happiest, and that's all a brother would ever ask for. To see the angel of his life treated as a Goddess by the man who claims to love her."

It was a heartfelt moment for me, watching Treyton play his seasonal match with another university, and every time he got a chance to spare, his addictive whiskeys watched me.

Grayson and I are still working on our sibling relationship slowly, and I trust this time around, our bond won't be a silk thread that knots in messy tangles of unfortunate emotions and twisted trusts.

"Ouch..." I yelled, glaring at Treyton, who stripped us under the shower. The steam collecting on the glass cubicle. "You hit me."

"You were not paying attention. Focus on me, Chipmunk. Look how I fuck my pretty pink pussy." His whiskeys darkened, and I felt weak in my limbs.

My chestnuts drink him, and his whiskeys slithers on me.

"I have eyes only for you, Treyton." My hands traced his chest, nails grazing his nipples, slowly, slowly, and slowly gliding down on his rigid abdominal muscles, touching the abs, and moving down with me on my knees in front of him. For his taking.

Water traced his muscular contour, and I caught the one dripping from his dick on my lips, licking the droplet as he watched me.

"Mouth open. Head tilted back," he ordered, anchoring my mouth to his erect cock with hands on the back of my head, gripping my wet locks.

He moaned my name, slipping inside my mouth, and my pussy spasmed, with warm heat flooding.

I moved, taking his length inside my mouth and adjusting after a few gag reflexes until the tip touched the back of my throat. The pleasure seeped in, and my other hand grabbed his thighs as he thrusts rapidly, at a merciless pace.

"My good little slut, taking my cock with such gratitude." He pushed deeper down my throat, and tears lined my lids.

"Mmmhhh..." I moaned with my mouth full.

"Touch yourself, my girl. Show me how much you're thankful for being fucked in your mouth by your God." His dirty teasing coming in deep breaths as he controlled his speed to not come inside my mouth, fucked me in ways I had no explanation for.

My hands slipped between my legs, and I dipped two fingers inside my pussy, quivering and playing with my clit from the other while Treyton fucked my mouth leisurely.

A cry left my lips, and I panted, trembling and sliding fingers in and out. The extreme stimulation of playing with my pussy and Treyton's dick inside my mouth made me come.

"Good girl," he patted my head, and helped me stand on my wobbly feet, while kissing me intensely, tasting my mouth engulfed in his remnants.

Holding my wrist up, he sucked my fingers, covered in my heat.

My heart bloomed, watching him staring as he sucked on my fingers, and grumble, "fucking delicious."

The hue creeping up my neck to my cheeks tinted them.

He turned me around and pushed me to the wall, separating my legs from behind and entering my starved pussy that wanted him just as much.

He left bite marks on my entire back and fucked me into the

wall like an animal. His dick filled me to the hilt, and my pussy swallowed every inch. Our hands entwined, and moans synched.

"Oh, God... Ahhh..." My eyes rolled back in my head, and I came undone.

Treyton kissed my shoulders, printing his smile on my skin, and changed our position.

"Thank your God, Chipmunk." His creepy voice instigates a feral animal inside me, hungry for his praise.

"Thank you, my God." One of the rules we've established of our own in our Master and Slave contract. I thank him after every fuck, addressing him as my God.

"Good girl, now your God will fuck you again, fill both your holes, and you'll scream another phrase of gratitude. Understood?" His growl low in octave made me obey.

"Yes, my God." I could sense his smile without looking at how much he appreciated me and the words of praise I have for him. That, too, he knows, is for our intense fucking because Treyton may not like power switches, but he loves the prankster in me dominating him in a chokehold. He calls it sexy.

He pushed his dick inside me, and I screamed the thank-you phrase.

His hips slapped against mine. My pussy clenching on him, the squelching sound of our tangled bodies, and his hand wrapped around my throat from behind, keeping me together on my feet and on my waist, giving him leverage to go deeper.

I panted and came undone again, my eyes rolled back in my head and saliva dripping from the corner of my mouth. He pulled out and widened my legs with his thighs nudged between. His hands parted my arse cheeks, and his thumb rotated over the seam of my arse-hole.

"Take my cock. Good girl," and he pushed inside. My hands were flat on the wall, and I stood on my tippy-toes. The violent thrusts overpowered the water sound from the shower, and he made me cum again, his one hand on my hips and the other playing with my sensitive clit.

He fucked me thoroughly until he pulled out and came on my arse. Both of us spent.

"You're incredible, Chipmunk." He turned me around and kissed me.

We somehow managed to clean and come out of the shower because the house bell was ringing frantic.

I opened the door and squealed, "welcome," hugging Dad, who glared at Treyton standing behind me.

"You lad, stop touching my daughter." He yelled, and Treyton's parents, standing behind the man of the evening with Hunter, Scarlett, Grayson, and Majesty, laughed at the charade.

"Congratulations, Oberon." Treyton went for a handshake, and both the males came to terms with each other.

I brought the chilled bottle of champagne for a toast, and Treyton helped me pour the glasses.

"I am happy to see, our Lyric is finally smiling after the healing therapy she took with a proper psychiatrist." The warm gaze of Lavender nourished a smile on everyone's face.

“Who thought we'd ever witness Treyton smitten." David made a snide remark.

"That's called pussy whipped," Hunter added, tossing a chocolate strawberry in his mouth.

"Shut up Hunter, I don't want to hear that about my sister," Grayson grumbled, taking the flute, I offered.

We gathered around and toasted for beautiful beginnings. It's rightfully the term for my gifted present.

"Cheers to our beautiful beginnings."

We all separated, taking our corners, and having a nice evening with friends and family.

However, when I glanced at Treyton watching me laugh at Majesty’s joke, I blushed. Excusing myself, I crossed the room to reach my man. As soon as Hunter saw his friend drifting away from their conversation, he gave me a sweet smile and quietly took his leave from Treyton’s side.

Treyton wrapped his hands around me and I couldn't speak a word. Without this man, I would've remained a liar. A mad pianist.

He came into my life and proved to me that existing for myself and him is all I need. All I want.

"My addictive whiskeys."

With him, there is a self-worth I have discovered.

"My Chipmunk."

I am the priority of my special someone. The god who became

my love letter to happiness.

EPILOGUE

"You're crazy." She giggled, and I licked her release on my lips, zipping her jeans.

"I am crazy. About you." I stole a quick kiss just after our quickie, and she responded, tasting herself on me.

With her, days are crazy. Not that I mind. But kidnapping her brother's girlfriend wasn't what I expected her to do, and her reply was, "I always wanted to kidnap someone and report them missing."

She is fucked up in her head.

"I didn't mean that, but okay. I take it." I gave up trying to make sense of it.

She kissed me for the last time before rushing out of the green room, and I exited, joining everyone on the ground, looking over the grand stage of our university's music festival.

She is performing this afternoon with Ciro. Her career has skyrocketed in these two years, and I've started investing and setting up my pharmaceutical company with Hunter. We both are growing, and there's no day normal, considering she is bored with the word *normal.*

"Stop smiling like a creep!" Scarlett elbowed me, and I ignored her. Focusing on the stage.

The artificial fog clouded the area, while the speakers blared with the background music as the centre of the stage rose an inch, and she appeared with a mic in her hand.

"Your girl," Hunter whispered over the loud cheering crowd, and I smiled wide, loving the sound of the words.

Yes, *my girl.*

We've come a long way, and I see us walking to the very forever every night we go to sleep, and every day I wake to see her beautiful face. One heck of a lucky bastard, I am.

She started singing, and the crowd went wild.

It's hilarious to witness how the same people who once hated her are dying to speak to her. But given her hands are full with me and her pranks, there is no room for another. Will never be.

Her seductive voice allured me. The siren sings beautifully. Everything about her was a rhythm strumming in my system.

He was a stranger.
A hunter in the dark.

I smirked at the lyrics. She eloquently sent a hidden message to me.

"I hear you, Chipmunk." I mouthed to her, our eyes on each other despite her moving with every lyric she whispered through her lips.

...He was a God of whiskeys in the burning hell...

My eyes dilated. "I know Chipmunk. I know."

...She was a sin in the witch's forbidden spell...

Ciro and Lyric were great on the stage as they ended, and I desperately wanted it to end. So I can steal her for our vacation. Precisely my jealous arse cannot come after every fucker drooling on my girl because then it'd be not a nice sight to see.

"Everyone. It's an emergency." Lyric shouted over the mic, and I closed my eyes, sensing another migraine.

"Uh-Oh." Everyone who knew her repeated in sync.

"There is a bomb in the ground. Do not panic."

The crowd shouted, and some started crying, thinking they were going to die.

I couldn't help but laugh, reading her mischievous smile, when she was forced to reveal it was a prank.

"Oh... And yes... Treyton Spade... I love you." Her ear-piercing voice made everyone groan when the speakers produced an unbearable sound.

Majesty went on the stage, snatched her mic, and dragged her away. All the while, I couldn't stop laughing.

When she is present, emotions take on a different meaning and definition. Living with her has given me a reason to smile a little bit more each day and a sense of what the meaning of life is.

To Be Continued...

BLACK COLLAR

I gulped, looking at him standing across the room. He was still the man I fell for. He was still the man with addictive whiskey eyes. He was still the God I was living for.

And yet, he was no longer the man to whom I vowed to spend the rest of my life on the altar.

Because in this union, Treyton Spade wasn't just my husband. He was a stranger, and I was his bride, bound in a relationship of convenience.

"Look, isn't it, Layla, Treyton's ex-girlfriend?" One of the ladies hummed among her friend group, and my eyes automatically found him looking at the gorgeous bombshell.

Layla Hart.

The girl, because of whom the man I worshipped fell out of love with me. And that doesn't even begin to explain the tragedy. To think, Layla Hart would be Nile Clifford's ex-wife.

A piece of news... This day is a lot special. Nile has been in asylum for eight years. It's been two years since I broke up with Treyton and a week since I married him. And, today, is the day the God insignia of Omen is established.

"Trust him." The heavy voice of David made me chuckle.

"You trust the one you love. We're strangers bound by a marriage contract." I reminded him, sipping my champagne.

"And what if I say, it's related to the unsolved mystery of your past."

Despite the brutal breakup I had, my heart begged me to believe it, even though my brain told me to deny it.

I smiled, swirling the content in my flute.

"Do you know what the funniest part of our story is, David? He fell for a girl who became obsessed with him."

"I do not understand." His confusion was the element I loved.

"I'm worried about your son. A woman is stalking him." Even though we broke up, I wasn't going to let anyone take away my God.

ACKNOWLEDGEMENT

This book was fun to write, and healing in so many ways. Red hands that abruptly secured a place in my head and my heart, with it's storyline and couple dynamic is special. And it always will be considering, how I was smiling with each line or crying with some deep emotions while creating Treyton and Lyric's story.

The characters were loudest and slowly, I started living so many of them in my head, it became senseless to shut the voices. Although, this wouldn't be possible without the people who supported me through every chapter of this book.

To begin with, my writing career itself would've never been possible, if my mother wouldn't have been the pillar that keep echoing in my ears, you can do.

Thanks, to my sisters, I was able to give beautiful memories and a fire spitting dynamic to Treyton and Lyric.

And not to forget, my friend Sara, without whom the hot Professor Nile could never have such a detailed syndicate running around. Without her I could've never been able to plot the secret society or work through the pressure if she wasn't there popping help with every insta message, be it day or night. So, thanks my love.

I'm equally grateful to my editor and supporter, who polished this book to finess, Halima. As much as she fell for Treyton and requested to find him in real life, she refined him and Lyric, so the world would be able to understand them and connect with them.

And thanks to all those readers who have given me a chance, I'll make sure to keep you all uncomfortable. Without you all my dream wouldn't be a reality, and an infinite possibility.

ABOUT AUTHOR

Isis Melantha loves to put a seal on her lips behind her computer screen and dissect codes for passion. Her crazy obsession with gaming, hacking, psychology, literature, traveling, and crime got twisted when she stumbled upon dark romance books and now apart from reading, she looks forward to telling the world a mystery of imagination that lies crooked and illegal in her head. Shaping the nastiest of men and sassiest of women. They know the dark secrets that she puts in her words. She hopes for her trauma and dark evil soul to find a home in the heart of the one who reads her books, while she's still on the journey to navigate her life and explore the world.

I am not your comfort author. I take pride in making you uncomfortable.

RBGW SERIES

Thanks for giving the world of RBGW Series a chance!

This series is my special love note to all those who love dark romances, and college romances, yet after cherishing each page still want more of it or maybe just one last sip...

And if you want more from this series and looking forward to the St. Evelyn Universities' devastatingly beautiful couples, then search no more. Just have patience and check out the books coming next in the series.

The RBGW Series
#1 Red Hands
#2 Blue Lips
#3 Green Eyes
#4 White Locks

CONNET WITH AUTHOR

Instagram @isis_melantha

Threads @isis_melantha

Twitter @isis_melantha

Goodreads @isis-melantha

Join my FB Reader's Group : Isis's Devils

Or Access every link through:
My Links

www.ingramcontent.com/pod-product-compliance
Ingram Content Group UK Ltd.
Pitfield, Milton Keynes, MK11 3LW, UK
UKHW041312190726
13845UKWH00025B/208

9 789334 018554